MIDDLETOWN

MIDDLETOWN

SARAH MOON

LEVINE QUERIDO

MONTCLAIR · AMSTERDAM · NEW YORK

This is an Arthur A. Levine book

Published by Levine Querido

LEVINE QUERIDO

www.levinequerido.com · info@levinequerido.com

Levine Querido is distributed by Chronicle Books LLC.

Copyright © 2021 by Sarah Moon · All rights reserved

Library of Congress Control Number: 2020937504

ISBN: 978-1-64614-042-8

Printed and bound in China

MIX
Paper from
responsible sources
FSC
www.fsc.org
FSC™ C144853

Published April 2021

First Printing

For my sister, Caitlin,
the banana to my peanut butter.

— 1 —

ELI WOKE UP when Anna's hot breath on her back suddenly stopped. She knew she was too big to be the little spoon, too old to share a bed with her sister, but on nights when Mom was out—and that was most nights lately—their small apartment felt too big and they curled up the same way that they had since Eli could remember, her chubby body curled tight, facing the wall, Anna's tall skinniness tracing a curve behind her. Eli heard Anna sigh; through her closed lids she could see the red and blue flashing lights dancing on the walls through the window.

"Damn it," Anna said as she slipped out of bed and threw on her black jeans and a tank top. One and a half minutes until the knock on the door. Eli's job was always the same. Stall. She wrapped a blanket around herself, grabbed a teddy bear from under her bed. Her job was to look young, sweet, and sleepy. She ran a hand through her short blond hair, hoping for some extra adorable points for bedhead. Anna's job was the opposite. She was applying mascara with one hand while tucking her hair behind her ear with the other. And there was the knock. Anna threw Eli a "one minute" sign from the bathroom. She finished her lip gloss and readjusted her boobs in the mirror. Another knock, and this time Anna nodded.

Eli's voice came out just right, about an octave higher and three shades more innocent. "Hello?"

"Police. Open the door, please."

"Yes, officer?" Eli said, going up to a squeak at the end of the word, faking a yawn as she opened the door. "Oh, hi Officer Sanders." Officer Sanders worked security at big events at the high school. Well, what were big events in Middletown, anyway.

"Hi Eli."

"Good evening, officer." Anna dropped the sexy act when she realized it was Officer Sanders. "Oh, hi. Eli, go back to bed."

Eli got back in bed, staring out the window at the lights shining into the room from the cop car below. The bed seemed to have gone cold just in the few minutes they'd been up. Normally, she listened to the sounds of Anna's best flirting, waiting to hear the sound of the fridge opening, a beer can popping. But Officer Sanders had known them both since they were each in first grade, had known Mom since *she* was in high school. They'd even gone on a few dates back in the day. This wasn't the first time he'd come to the house to tell them that Mom messed up, again. Hopefully he'd take pity on them, not call Social Services until morning (or better yet, not at all). A minute more of Anna's high voice and his low one, and then the door closed. Eli listened to the heavy boots clomping down the stairs.

"She's not coming home tonight," Anna said, standing in the doorway, arms hooked around her back as she took off the push-up bra and slid back into pajama pants.

Anna sat on the bed, her legs resting on either side of Eli, her hands pushing down just a little hard on Eli's head. They watched the red and blue lights fade as the officer drove off. "Drunk tank?" asked Eli.

"Yeah, till morning."

"Then what?"

"Then, we'll see."

"Is he calling Social Services?"

"He didn't say. Let's hope no news is good news for now."

—2—

IN THE MORNING, Anna seemed back to her regular seventeen-year-old self. Her black hair was in a ponytail, and she was wearing a black tank top, a black hoodie zipped up to right under her boobs, black jeans, and black boots. She'd been dressing like this since September, a radical transformation from the French-braided, floral-printed soccer princess she'd been until then. Eli still missed that old soccer-princess-Anna from time to time. She was nicer, less grumpy, fought less with Mom, and she liked to hang out with Eli, even though Eli was just her baby sister.

All of that changed a few months ago, and since then, even when Anna made an effort to come home and hang out with Eli, it was like there was a boulder sitting between them that had never been there before. Eli tried not to think that it was anything she'd done— that maybe they'd just gotten too different. It wasn't like they didn't talk or they fought all the time; it was just that something had changed and neither of them could figure out how to change it back.

Anna shooed Eli out of the bathroom as she traced black eyeliner into the corners of her eyelids. Eli pulled on the same jeans from the last three days and her favorite red striped shirt. She added her gray hoodie and a baseball hat.

"You're not going to be able to hide your boobs forever, you know," said Anna, watching her from the bathroom.

"Sorry I don't show them off for the whole school every day, or for Jaaaaaason, like some people."

"Shut up, PB."

"Seriously, you've been wearing boobalicious tank tops every day for two weeks, and jeans that you practically have to glue on to your body. Has he even talked to you yet?"

"What do you know? Nothing, that's what. In love with your best friend."

"At least she knows I'm alive."

"She likes boys, kid. Sorry."

"How would you know? Are you one?"

"You're such a child," Anna said, flicking off the light in the bedroom on her way out. "By the way, if you really want her to notice you, you might consider showering more than every three days, stinker."

"Whatever," said Eli to no one in the dark bedroom.

In the kitchen, Eli washed dishes as Anna got out bowls for cereal.

"Of-freaking-course. No milk," Anna said, slamming the door to the fridge.

"I'll just eat mine dry."

"That's so gross." Anna poured some water from the tap into her bowl.

"That's grosser."

They sat at the kitchen table and chewed.

"When do you think they'll let her out?" asked Eli, throwing a Mini-Wheat into her mouth.

"I don't know," said Anna. "Or care."

"I do," Eli said. "I want to know she's okay."

"Mom's fine. Mom's hungover. Mom'll sleep it off and grab an egg-and-cheese, come home, sleep some more, and then Mom'll do it again tonight. Honestly, you shouldn't worry about her. It's not like she's worried about us."

Eli looked down and away. She knew Anna liked to think of herself as Eli's protector, but Anna had a way of hurting her like hardly anyone else could.

"Come on, kid. We're going to be late," Anna said, flipping Eli's baseball cap off her head and ruffling her hair. Apology not accepted, Eli thought.

Hoover Junior High and Middletown High School were a half mile and a world apart. The girls took the bus together. Eli got off first, and Anna headed up the hill to the high school, where, Eli'd been told, everything would be better. This seemed unlikely.

Eli waited outside for Javi and Meena. It was always the kids who lived closest, the ones in the fancy Laurel Crest neighborhood just down the street, who got to school last. And then teachers wanted to yell at Eli for arriving five minutes late when it was the bus's fault, not hers. But today it wasn't going to be the bus's fault; it was going to be Javi's and Meena's. If they didn't hurry up, she'd be late for first-period English and Ms. Russo would say, "Third time this month, Eliza," and give her detention, because that was just how Ms. Russo was. But if she went in without them, she'd have to deal with Kevin. He would be waiting where he was always waiting; she could see his baseball cap through the window in the door. If she was alone, he'd follow her down the hall saying, "Hi boy, good morning boy, how are you boy," and try to push her into the boys' bathroom. If she was with Javi and Meena, they'd all flip him off together and saunter off to class. It was amazing what being best friends with the prettiest girl in the eighth grade could do. And Meena was just that—everyone knew it but her.

Everyone also knew Javi was gay, and not just that he was gay, but that he was a gay, Puerto Rican, chubby classics nerd with the right answers and thick glasses and a love of the ablative. In any other school he'd be a walking target, more so even than Eli. But here, he was also the principal's son, and not even Kevin was stupid enough to mess with him. Eli liked Principal Calderón and wished that the principal's powers of protection applied to her too. They gave Javi a shine of confidence that Eli hoped would one day rub off on her.

Eli nervously eyed her phone: exactly one minute until the late bell. She weighed her choices—Kevin and his stupid hat and the boys' bathroom, or waiting for these two fools to finally show up and probably getting detention. Either way, she'd be late, and if she could avoid Kevin, detention would be worth it. Plus, she'd probably have it with Javi and Meena anyway. She opened their group text.

Where are you guys? Russo's gonna kill me.

As she pressed send, Javi's hand appeared on her shoulder. "Sorry, E, our diva slept in. I had to go in and wake her myself, okurrrr?" Ever since the new season started, Javi talked like he was in the workroom of *RuPaul's Drag Race*, despite the fact that he knew a total of zero other gay people (besides Eli) and that the closest thing to a drag queen he'd ever seen in person was a bunch of bagpipers in their kilts at the Memorial Day Parade.

"Some of us need our beauty rest, Javi. We can't all wake up like Beyoncé."

Javi pushed the door open and walked through, the hallway his personal catwalk. Meena went next in her everyday jeans and T-shirt that, on her, looked somehow elegant, effortless, and cool. Eli followed behind. She could be their third wheel, but Meena would say, "No way; we're a triangle, that's all," and Javi would say, "Yeah, a pink one," and Meena and Eli would laugh and roll their eyes and shout, "That's so gay!" at him until they were all laughing and had no idea why. They never made Eli feel like their less-cool, less-popular counterpart, though she knew that's exactly what she was. On bad days, Eli wondered why they hung out with her anyway.

Eli's theory was that all middle schools are a special kind of punishment, a place to jail kids while they go through puberty. Hoover was particularly cruel, housing only seventh and eighth graders—a deserted island keeping pubescent kids trapped away from the precious, innocent sixth graders and from the freedoms of high school. Meena and Javi went up to sixth grade at Country Independent before their parents sent them to "meet real people" at Hoover. Eli wasn't one of the real people they met until this time last year, as if by magic, in health class on a Friday, last period. Mr. Johnson was the basketball coach/health teacher, and he was much more comfortable on the court than in the classroom. They were playing Puberty Jeopardy, which is a terrible idea no matter what, but an even worse one with seventh graders on a Friday. When he read the question, "The sac of skin that protects the testicles and regulates their temperature," Kevin said, "Uh, what is your mom?" When Eli muttered, "No, Kevin, what is *your* mom," Javi looked over at her with a raised eyebrow and a smile. Everything went predictably to hell, and Mr. Johnson yelled, cajoled, and finally gave up, sat down, and read the paper.

"You're funny," said Javi.

"I mean, I can do better than a 'your mom' joke, but since Kevin can't, I figured I should play fair."

"He'd be diabolical if he wasn't so dumb."

"I think he may be both."

"True."

"I'm Eli."

"Javier. My friends call me Javi, and you're one of them now. Cute, funny homosexuals are my cup of tea. I'm not making any assumptions, of course."

Eli laughed. "No, none at all."

"Meena." Javi poked the girl sitting next to him. "This is our new friend Eli. Eli, this is Meena, the only heterosexual in this godforsaken place worth knowing."

"I'm flattered," said Meena. "It's nice to meet you. I hope to live up to the title of worthy heterosexual friend for you as well." It was immediate with Meena, like something out of a movie. Even in that horrible, smelly health class, Meena's smile was all the things in all the pop songs—a ray of sunshine, a shot to her heart, a flip in her stomach. The fluorescent lights seemed to make a halo over her long, dark hair. The three of them started talking that afternoon and basically hadn't stopped since. That was one year ago. This morning was just one of the many in the last year during which Eli had waited for Javi and Meena to stroll to school arm-in-arm, scooping her up on the way. Every single detention had been worth it, though Eli made sure to keep it just under the number that required a parent-teacher conference. She didn't want Mom to come to school.

In History, Eli's stomach started to rumble. One look in her bag made her smile. Anna might be all goth and boobs lately, but that didn't stop her sister from throwing some Oreos into Eli's backpack. She snuck one quietly when Mr. Simmons had his back turned. Eli swore she heard someone oink at her. It was quiet enough to be anonymous, loud enough to make Spencer and Jack laugh and make Eli blush. She wished that she could stop blushing forever. If she had one superpower, it'd be utter control of every physical manifestation of her emotions. No more sweating when she was nervous, blushing when she was embarrassed, or crying when she was angry.

Spencer's laugh made Mr. Simmons turn around. "Really, guys? I can't even write on the board without antics? Really?"

The Oreo had only made Eli's stomach louder, hungry for more. It was going to be a long day until lunch.

That afternoon, after the bell rang at the end of last period, Javi, Meena, and Eli piled into their favorite spot, the faculty bathroom on the third floor. It was supposed to be locked to students, and you were supposed to get a special key from the nurse if you needed it, but Javi had taped the lock open months ago, and they'd been gathering there ever since. Javi was going off (and off and off) about his mother's new boyfriend, who he wasn't supposed to talk about at school.

"What did Doofus do now?" Eli asked as she took her spot by the hand dryer.

"Well, first of all, he keeps calling me 'Princess,' which is cute when you guys do it, but you can tell he's just doing it to mess with me. Never in front of my mom, of course. She just thinks I'm trying to break them up. Which, obvi, would be great, but I only feel that way *because he's a jerk*. I don't have to make up his jerkishness—there's plenty to go around."

"It's your castle. You should tell him to call you 'Queen.'"

"I really should."

"Let's go, late people," nudged Meena, jumping off the sink.

Russo had given Eli detention; Javi and Meena had gotten it too. Eli didn't care; in some way, walking down the hall together to detention was the best part of her day. Mrs. Gibbons held her head in one hand and a red pen in the other, shaking her head in disbelief—either over the amount of papers she had to correct or the number of wrong answers her students were giving. She didn't even look up from her pile of worksheets when Meena asked Eli if she wanted to come over for dinner. Dinner at Meena's house was always a good idea: her mom tied aprons around both of their waists and put them to work. Eli chopped and Meena stirred and there was classical music in the background, the sounds of her little brother and sister running around in the yard floating through the windows. Her dad came by and kissed Meena's cheek, asked how her day was. "Hey sport," he always said to Eli, awkward but kind. It was like having dinner with a Disney family.

On days like today, though, Mom usually came in tired and worried, covering it all with a big smile and pizza. "Oh my girls," she'd say. "I love you both so much. My girls, my girls." Anna would probably roll her eyes and storm into her bedroom, the way she'd taken to doing lately, but Eli would sit on the couch with Mom, watching TV with her until Mom fell asleep and Eli shook her to go to bed. Her phone would vibrate with a text while she was sitting on the couch. It would be Anna texting from her room.

I don't know why you bother.

Eli wouldn't reply.

"I can't come tonight, sorry," Eli whispered back to Meena, hating to squander time with Meena and her magic family. "Maybe next week?"

—3—

"WHERE THE HELL have you been? I texted you." The phrase shot off Anna's tongue the second Eli walked through the door, like it had been waiting right behind her teeth to jump out of her mouth.

"Easy, killer. My phone died," Eli said. "It's five. I had detention, and then I came home. What's your problem?"

"I was worried, okay? So sue me. Sorry for caring." She threw herself on the couch with too much force.

"Yeah . . . okay . . ." said Eli, looking around. "Where's Mom?"

"She's not here."

"Yeah, I see that. Where is she?"

"How should I know?" Her hands went from the pockets of her hoodie, to her lap, to redoing her ponytail in under a minute.

"Anna."

"She's not coming home, okay? The guidance counselor pulled me out of last period. Mom's been arrested. Like, *arrested* arrested. Not like last time. This isn't a drunk tank thing. She was driving last night when she got pulled over. *Driving*, Eli."

"Yeah, and?"

"And drunk driving is a crime, and it's not like this is the first time she's done it, or even the first time she's been caught for it, and so, let me correct myself. I do know where Mom is. Mom's in jail. And she's staying there this time."

"You don't know that."

"You're right. I don't know that. Maybe they're going to let her out to come home and beg for our forgiveness with a freaking pizza. You live in a dream world, kid, you really do."

Eli said nothing, stomped into her room, and slammed the door.

"It's always up to me," she heard Anna mutter through the thin walls, and then muffled bass, probably PJ Harvey—Anna had been listening to her on repeat. Eli threw herself facedown onto her bed, not bothering to take off her shoes or even her backpack. The weight of it against her felt good, pushed her down further, like heavy armor between her and the rest of the day.

It wasn't that Eli didn't know that Anna was right. Anna seemed to think that Eli always forgave Mom because she was childish or naïve, too dumb to know better, too dumb to realize that this happened again and again and again. Eli forgave her because she's Mom, because even if your Mom is a drunk, she's still your mom, and what else can you do? You could hide under black clothes and a snarl like Anna, but that didn't seem to keep Anna from needing Mom any more than Eli did. And so Eli forgave her. Again and again and again. The tears came in as the sun set through her windows and the room grew dark. She wasn't crying hard; she barely noticed she was crying at all. It was just the day's way of making its peace with her. Tears leaked out of her eyes and onto her sheets and before she knew it, she was asleep.

Eli didn't hear Anna come in. But she noticed the smell of something like dinner cooking. It smelled warm and tomato-y.

"PB," Anna said, shaking her shoulder. "PB, wake up. I made us a feast. Well, I made us spaghetti. Or macaroni. I made us macaroni with spaghetti sauce. Let's call it macaroni di tomato à la Anna. Get up."

"You suck." Eli said, lifting her face from the sheets damp with tears and drool.

"I do, a little. I'm sorry. Come eat my crappy food that I prepared with all my suckiness and all my love. And take off your backpack. And your sneakers, gross."

Eli kicked them off, shrugged off her bag, and followed her sister to the table.

"So, what happens now?" she asked, lifting a forkful of spaghettaroni to her mouth.

"Now, I figure out how to keep us together," Anna said. "Here, it needs salt."

TOGETHER. OF COURSE they would be together. Eli and Anna, Peanut Butter and Banana. But of course Anna was right, who would leave a seventeen-year-old and a thirteen-year-old on their own for who-knows-how-long? No one knew how many nights they'd already been on their own, how many weekends Mom just went missing, how many times Anna had made something out of nothing for dinner. But no judge would say, "Sure, kids, you seem to have this under control." They both knew that—and knew that it was a miracle that they'd gotten these two days without a social worker showing up. The hearing was scheduled for three o'clock the next afternoon. If Eli could manage

not to get detention, she'd make it there right on time.
She sent a text to Javi and Meena in the morning:

Don't be late, assholes. Detention = death.

She ate a spoonful of peanut butter and threw on
her backpack.

"Banana, are you coming?"

"Yes. God!" They headed down the stairs together.
They walked down the street together. They waited for
the bus together. *Together*. She tried not to think that
word.

"Peanut, I've got this. Don't worry."

"I'm not worried."

"Sure you're not." Anna squeezed her shoulder as
they got on the bus. They rode the rest of the way in
silence. Eli got up at her stop and Anna said, "I'll see you
at the hearing at three. And then I'll see you at home."

"See you," Eli said. "Love—"

"Don't. I mean, I do too, but don't." Eli nodded
and waved as she got off the bus. She was relieved to
see Javi and Meena waiting there for her.

"Thanks, guys."

"What's the emergency?"

"No emergency."

"Mom on your case for detention?" Javi asked.
"Mine is particularly displeased."

"Mine too," said Meena.

"Totally," mumbled Eli as they walked down the hall, middle fingers high, past the open-mouthed Kevin obviously watching Meena's butt as they went past.

At 2:40, Javi and Eli were in math together. Eli stared at the clock, at her phone, at the clock.

"What's wrong?" Javi whispered.

Eli wanted to tell him; she knew that all the gears turning rapidly inside her were starting to send smoke out of her ears, that Javi could tell just by looking at her that something was wrong. But how do you explain to your friend who has spent the morning complaining about how his mom is really on him about family bonding that your mom is in jail? As far as Eli could tell, you didn't.

"I've got somewhere to be."

"A woman of mystery, eh? I'm into it."

Eli threw him a quick smile. "My mom's waiting for me."

The bell rang, and Eli was standing with her backpack on before it was done with its three loud blasts. Mr. Hendrix was mid-sentence, but Eli couldn't care today.

"Tell Meena I said bye. See you tomorrow." And she was out the door before Mr. Hendrix could say, "Class is over when I say it's over, young lady."

The courthouse was only a few blocks from school, in "downtown" Middletown, which was only a few blocks to begin with. Middletown was nestled off a stretch of highway between nothing and not much. It had been a mill town once upon a time, as every Middletown Elementary student learns on their annual visit to the no-longer-really-a-mill Middletown Mill. It wasn't a mill town anymore, just a town town, with a grocery store, a couple of gas stations, some fancy houses, and some apartment buildings pushed right at of the edge of town where they wouldn't offend anyone's eyesight.

Eli paused on the courthouse steps and looked for Anna. 2:52. She'd wait for three more minutes. Eli looked at her watch only to find that it was still 2:52. She texted Anna. Nothing. 2:53. A text from Meena on the group chat:

You took off like a bat out of hell.

She texted back:

That place is hell. Had to do a thing for my mom. See you tomorrow.

2:54. These were minutes she could be spending with Mom. She did one last scan for a black ponytail, black tank top, black jeans, black hoodie moving quickly down the block. Nothing.

The courthouse was surprisingly elegant by Middletown standards. More marble than Eli'd ever seen in one place, enormous windows with gold frames and a high ceiling that made her footsteps echo. It was still Middletown, though, so she found the room easily enough; it was one of two, and the only one with people in it. Also, Mom was waiting outside. So that was a clue. She looked tired. Eli threw herself into her arms without a word.

"Hi, my baby," Mom said, squeezing her tight.

"Hi."

"Let me look at you."

"I'm fine, Mom," Eli said, pulling away so that Mom could see that it was true. "We're fine."

"Where's Anna?"

"I don't know. But she'll be here. Don't worry."

"I'm so sorry, Eli. I didn't . . ."

"It's okay, Mom. We're okay." Eli noticed a woman with a briefcase by her mother's side. She was wearing a black suit and heels, a lawyer for sure.

"Eli, this is the public defender, Ms. Matthews. This is my daughter Eliza."

"Hi."

"Hi Eliza. We're going to do everything we can for your mom, okay hon?" Her voice was sugary and distracted. A pit opened in the bottom of Eli's stomach.

"Carrie, it's time to go in." Ms. Matthews opened the door for Mom, and Eli followed behind her.

"You can sit in the row right behind us, okay big girl?" Ms. Matthews said as they walked to the front of the room. Eli grinned a ferocious grin as she dug her nails into her palm to keep from yelling. This wasn't the time.

The bailiff called the court to order, and they all rose for Judge Lee. She was younger than Eli thought she would be, with black curls piled on top of her head and kind eyes. This all seemed like a good sign. But Anna's absence sucked all of the luck out of good signs. Where was she? *Together.* She'd promised. Eli bit her lip just hard enough to get herself to remember: You can't believe what people tell you. How many times do you have to learn?

In the row in front of her, Mom stood to answer Judge Lee's questions. She said her age (thirty-four), her plea (guilty), her employment (secretary, which had been true but probably wasn't now), and how many children she had (two; where is Anna, where is Anna, where is Anna). The judge went over the facts of Mom's case—this was the second time this month that Mom had been caught driving with more than twice the legal limit of alcohol in her system. As far as Judge Lee could tell, Mom was headed to a third any day now, and three strikes meant real jail time. Jail wasn't the worst thing in her future, Judge Lee explained, because obviously if she kept going the way she was going, she could kill herself or someone else, and she could lose her kids. Eli bit her lip again, this time to keep herself from crying. The best option, Judge Lee said plainly, was for Mom to go to rehab. Today.

"Could the girls stay with their father?" the judge asked.

Their father. Common mistake. They didn't know Anna's father, the boy who got Mom knocked up when she was sixteen, younger then than Anna was now, but when they were little Anna would tell Eli stories about him—long and thin like her, his head of wavy black hair and piercing blue eyes. He was a firefighter, or maybe a movie star. He was looking for her, she was sure. Anna didn't talk about that anymore, but Eli couldn't help but notice her slight double take at tall, blue-eyed, dark-haired men, at the diner or on the bus, like part of her still believed he was waiting for her.

Eli's dad was Sam, and both sisters' lives were divided into two time periods: Before Sam Left (BSL) and After Sam Left (ASL). Eli had all of Sam's sweetness, and his thick, blond hair. Eli had heard Anna tell the story a million times—how Sam had come and rescued Mom from her loneliness, from her single-mom-ness, from being-twenty-years-old-and-having-a-toddler-ness, and had filled their tiny apartment with his particular Sam sunshine, with his strong arms and his big smile. And then Mom got pregnant with Eli. Sam would crow about his pack of girls, his house full of women to love and protect, all sorts of sweet and macho shit. According to Anna, then Mom started going out more and more at night, leaving Sam at home with a crying baby and a four-year-old, until one morning they all woke up, and he was gone. All Eli knew was that things were perfect, and then she was born.

"No, they can't stay with their father," Mom said.

"A relative, then?" Judge Lee asked. "You'll be gone for a minimum of ninety days, and the girls need to be with a guardian or they'll be placed in foster care."

The door to the courtroom swung open, the *click-clack* of heels on the linoleum hushing the room. A blond woman walked to the front, her hair in a tight bun, floral blouse perfectly ironed under a light purple sweater. Her small gold cross caught the light as she passed down the aisle. Only if you were sitting where Eli was could you see the tiny tattoo of a sun, just behind her right ear where her blond hair was tucked. Same as Anna's.

"Your Honor, my name is Lisa Reynolds. I'm the girls' aunt. I'll be happy to stay with them while my sister gets the help she needs." Mom's head jerked back in surprise. The last time any of them had seen Aunt Lisa was that bad Christmas years ago, and they hadn't spoken since, but Eli was pretty sure that however long it had been, Aunt Lisa wasn't now young, blond, and getting matching tattoos with Anna. Mom looked quickly to Eli. Eli tried to keep her face neutral, no smiling, no laughing at these ridiculous circumstances or her big sister's crazy ideas; she just nodded. *Together.* Judge Lee was quiet for a long time, looking "Aunt Lisa" up and down.

"You're quite young to be anyone's aunt," she finally said.

"Twenty-three, Your Honor, and more than happy to take care of my nieces. I've known them all their lives. We're quite close." Judge Lee nodded slowly, her head cocked to the side like she was trying to understand a piece of strange art, or like she was trying to catch a teenager in a lie. She sighed.

"Ms. Reynolds, do you agree to have your sister care for your children in your absence?" Mom looked long and sad at Anna, who nodded just slightly. *Together.*

"Of course. Thank you."

"And, Ms. Reynolds," she looked now at Aunt Lisa, "Where are you living?" Only Eli could see the gears turning quickly inside of Anna. Well, maybe Mom could see them too.

"My sister has come all the way from Vermont, Your Honor, she's recently graduated from Oxbridge College and works in the area. Lisa, thank you for coming all this way. Why don't you stay at the house while you have the girls?" Anna nodded solemnly.

"That'd be perfect. 56 Stanton Court, 4G, right?"

"Yes." Judge Lee looked first at Mom and then at "Aunt Lisa," curious, maybe even suspicious, but resigned.

"Very well. Expect to be hearing from Social Services regularly," Judge Lee warned.

"I'm happy to be able to help, Your Honor."

—5—

"WOW," SAID ELI afterward, sitting on the court-house steps next to Anna.

"That was way, way too close. Did you see how she was looking at me? She could tell, PB."

"I know, but then she was all 'Very well,' so we're fine."

"This time." They sat silently for a few minutes, trying not to think about next time.

"Here's my question, Aunt Lisa—what next? And also, where did you get a fake ID?"

"Next, we go home. And none of your business."

Anna had given a fake address in Vermont, some made up street in Oxbridge (if the name of the town was even real). When they asked for an ID, she handed one over, adding calmly, "Sorry, just moved. Don't have a Vermont ID yet." Eli tried not to show her surprise, willing her eyebrows to stay in place and her mouth to stay shut. The only real thing Anna gave them was her phone number; hopefully a few chats with "Aunt Lisa" would buy some time with Social Services. That was how they were going to do this then, moment by moment. Not much of a plan, but they'd gotten through the past thirteen and seventeen years this way. They could make it through ninety days. Right?

The walk home was a silent one, buses pushing past the girls, dousing them with occasional showers of exhaust. Sunset painted downtown Middletown purple. It almost looked pretty.

"This is weird," Eli said as they walked into the dark apartment.

"Yeah," said Anna, sitting on the couch.

"I mean, it's not like she's usually here. It's just weird knowing . . ."

"That she won't be."

"Exactly."

"Well, at least you know that tonight you won't get woken up by a cop knocking on the door."

"Still, though."

"I've got to get out of this drag," said Anna, heading to her bedroom and taking off the mysterious, preppy clothes from a long-ago version of herself that she'd dug up from the deep recesses of her closet. She reappeared in new-Anna drag, all black, with her new blond ponytail tied high at the top of her head. She looked like a misfit toy—all the pieces smashed and put together wrong.

"Peanut, I know we'll figure this out. But."

"We'll figure it out."

"What the hell are we going to do?" they asked each other, themselves, the walls. Anna drew her knees to her chest. Eli chewed her fingernails.

"Quit that. Let's find something to eat that's not attached to your body."

"Picky, picky."

The girls went into the kitchen. Anna checked the cabinets and Eli checked the freezer. They each emerged victorious—Eli held a freezer-burned hot dog package, Anna dug up a bag of sour-cream-and-onion potato chips.

"A feast," said Anna. They high-fived.

After dinner, they watched TV until they fell asleep, Eli slumped against Anna's knees, Anna splayed on the couch.

In the morning, it was hot dogs for breakfast, their red, rubbery bodies much less appealing the second time around.

"Are we going to eat hot dogs for the next ninety days?" asked Eli.

"If we're lucky. We don't have any more." Eli looked at her, eyes wide. "Don't ask, Eli. I don't know what we're going to do yet, okay? I'll figure something out."

"Did the lawyer give you Mom's stuff yesterday?"

"Yeah, her wallet's empty. Shocker."

"And her car keys?"

"Yes, my little miscreant. We've got wheels."

"Good. You can drive me to school. What about credit cards?"

"Like Mom has credit cards that aren't maxed out. And we're taking the bus. I don't want to draw anybody's attention. We have to act normal."

Eli got up from the table and went into Mom's bedroom.

"PB, come on, we've got to go. Stop screwing around."

"Give me a minute."

Anna went into the bathroom, probably redoing her cat-eye makeup (for the second time). Eli barged in with a bag full of cash.

"Eli, where the hell did you get this?"

"The envelope at the top of the shelf in mom's closet under her old sweaters."

"Jesus, you are such a snoop! How did you even know this was there?"

"I didn't snoop. I put it there."

Anna turned around and faced her little sister. "Eli, no joke—have you been stealing from Mom? I'm supposed to be the bad one, and even I think that's pretty messed up."

"It's not stealing."

Anna pursed her dark red lips and raised a single black eyebrow. "What is it then?"

"I was saving it. For her. The first Tuesday of the month, Mom gets paid. She cashes the check, brings it home. While she's sleeping, I take twenty dollars and put it in this bag. I do it whenever she has a little extra cash. It's just twenty bucks. You know, for a rainy day."

Anna shook her head. "Little sister, I'm pretty sure that is stealing, but it's also a very, very good idea. How much do you have in there?"

"Nine hundred and sixty dollars."

"Holy shit, Eli, how long have you been doing this?"

"Since I was nine."

Anna shook her head. Eli knew that Anna had always tried to protect her, but even at nine, she knew more than nine-year-olds should. "I don't know how long it'll last us, but it's certainly a lot of hot dogs," Anna said. "Meet me at the store after school. We'll go grocery shopping."

"Can we get something other than hot dogs?"

"Anything you want."

—6—

ELI DIDN'T HEAR Anna honking outside school at three. She was talking with Javi and Meena, who were both bemoaning the states of their upcoming weekends.

"Camping with Mom and King Douchebag—can you believe it? Since when do we camp? She's really gone crazy with this one." Javi always talked about his mom's boyfriend like he was a temporary annoyance, but they'd been together for months, and Eli's bet was on him moving in before the end of the school year. She didn't dare tell Javi that, though.

"Indians don't camp," said Meena.

"Neither do Puerto Ricans! But Mr. Whitebread says it'll be good bonding. Kill me, please."

"I would, but I have to go to a wedding. So, you know, see you guys in like a month and a half."

"What?" exclaimed Eli, more alarmed than she wanted to be at the thought of not seeing Meena for so long.

"Relax—I'm kidding. Indian weddings are just really long, that's all. We'll be there forever. Eli, isn't that your sister?"

"Anna?"

"Yeah, over there honking at us and pointing at you?"

"I've got to go, guys. I'll see you Monday. Good luck in the woods, and at the wedding. Come back to me!" She hoped she sounded carefree and funny, but she wasn't really either of those things. She was wondering what Meena would wear to the wedding; she was thinking about dancing, and Meena's hips. "Come back to me" is exactly what she meant.

"Jesus Christ, earth to Eli!" said Anna, beckoning Eli over to the car.

"Sorry, I didn't see you."

"Of course you didn't because, *you only have eyeeees for herrrr,*" crooned Anna. "Get in."

"Anyway, I thought you said we couldn't use the car," said Eli as they pulled out of the parking lot, just one in the sea of buses and soccer mom and sports vans.

"I said we couldn't draw attention to ourselves. There's a bunch of parents picking up their kids here right now. Who's to say I'm not just a loving mother taking my daughter to a dentist appointment?"

"Or an abandoned child taking her little sister grocery shopping with money she's stolen from their drunken mother."

"Equally possible."

At the grocery store, Anna and Eli took turns pushing the cart. When it was Eli's turn she ran and jumped on the back, sliding down the aisle.

"Could you try not be such a child?" Anna said, with her practiced exhausted tone.

"Could you try not to be where fun goes to die?" asked Eli, tossing two bags of cookies into the cart, double-stuffed and regular.

"Let's make dinner," said Anna pensively.

"Duh, that's why we're here," Eli said, tossing chips into the cart while Anna stared into space.

"No, like real dinner."

"What do you know how to make?"

"Well, nothing, but how hard can it be? What do you want?"

"For real?"

"Sure."

"Let's make pizzas."

"What else?"

"Lasagna?"

The girls raced through the aisles, splitting up ingredients and meeting back at the cart with zucchini and sauce, cheeses and noodles, pepperoni and dough. Anna was pushing the cart to the register when Eli ran off for one more thing.

"We've got everything, Eli. I even got you pancake mix!"

"Hang on!"

Anna was unloading the cart when Eli returned a few seconds later with a bouquet of purple flowers in her hand.

"What's this for?"

"Because it's nice. Sometimes it's nice to be nice."

Anna smiled for what seemed like the first time in days.

"Sure, kid."

The total came to $158.56, and Eli tried not to think about the fact that this was enough food for a week and not much more. She could see hot dogs in their future if she looked closely. Anna handed over the cash, while Eli pretended to be oblivious, engrossed in the latest sex scandal featuring an actress on a TV show she'd never heard of and her brother/manager.

When they got home, the apartment hadn't changed since the morning, of course. But suddenly Eli could see it for what it was. Dirty, small, airless. The cracks in the walls seemed darker; the dishes in the sink seemed covered in grime that hadn't been there this morning. There seemed, suddenly, to be a fine film on the kitchen table, and when was the last time somebody swept the floor?

"We can't live like this," Anna said, putting the groceries on the counter.

Anna put on music, and they went to work on the kitchen. Eli washed dishes and wiped down the counters while Anna cleaned the table, putting the piles of old mail on her mother's bed, and then swept and mopped the floor. Eli cleaned the windows. Anna took a cotton swab to the baseboards. She cut the flowers and put them in water.

"Starting to look like a home in here."

"Yeah, somebody else's," Eli said, laughing. Sweaty and tired, Anna leaned her head on her sister's shoulder as Siouxsie and the Banshees blasted through the speakers.

"It's like a hurricane came through here," Eli said.

"That's called your mother."

"I hope you're not planning to go chase boys this weekend, Banana. We've got cleaning to do."

"For you, PB, I will forgo the pursuit of the peen for just this weekend."

"So kind of you, my loving sister."

"Please help me chop this pepperoni and prepare for my new life of celibacy."

"You are disgusting."

"And I'm all you've got. So get to work, and don't be stingy with the cheese."

The house filled with the smell of dough and hot tomato sauce, melted cheese and the vague sweetness of Eli's purple flowers. They sat at the kitchen table and ate their pizza in hungry silence.

"So, what are you going to do about this Meena thing?" Anna asked.

"Love her from afar and wait for the day I meet another gay in this cowtown?"

"You'll end up a nun."

"Thanks, very supportive."

"Maybe you should tell her how you feel."

"Maybe I should tell Jason the Leather Jacket how you feel about him and his peen."

"Don't you worry about me. Jason, his jacket, and the rest of him will soon be mine. TV?"

"TV."

The rest of the night faded into blue and purple lights shining from the TV onto their faces. Episode after episode of *The Walking Dead*, because it turns out zombies are soothing when everything else feels like the end of the world. The sisters fell asleep on top of each other, empty Oreo packages glistening in the glow of the screen.

Eli woke to the smell of pancakes, and the sound of Anna banging pots in the kitchen and playing My Bloody Valentine very, very loudly.

"Wow," Eli yawned, her blond hair a lion's mane. Or a rat's nest.

"Good morning, bedhead."

"Who are you and what have you done with my sister?"

"Haha. Funny. Do you want these or not?"

"Chocolate chips?"

"Duh."

"Then, duh, I want them."

Eli couldn't remember the last weekend that they'd both spent at home. Ever since Anna's radical transformation into a dark-souled goth, she'd spent every weekend trying to work her way into Jason's leather jacket, so Eli would try to get a night or two at Meena's or Javi's so she wouldn't feel Anna's absence so much. This weekend, though, the girls stayed home, making it home. They cleaned up from breakfast, Eli washing dishes and Anna drying. They battled the living room now, vacuuming the worn carpet until it was more like blue and less like gray. Eli cleared the coffee table, dumping yet another heap of mail on Mom's bed. One envelope caught her eye. She tucked it into her back pocket for later.

Anna vacuumed the couch; she even got under the couch. They took on the bathroom together, emptying trash, cleaning the toothpaste stains off the mirror, scrubbing down surfaces and erasing stains from who-knows-what-was-there. Their respective pigsties were next. That's what Mom called them when she noticed.

Anna's room had gone under rapid renovation this year, along with her transformation into the goth girl whose goals certainly didn't involve cleats. One Saturday after practice, Eli had been sitting on the couch when Anna burst through the front door. Eli tried to ask her what was wrong, but Anna just slammed the door and blared music for the rest of the afternoon. When she came out, she had an overflowing trash bag—Eli could make out the green of her uniform and the shiny gold of her trophies.

"I swear to god, Eli, if you ask me a single question right now, I will never speak to you again," Anna said as she stomped back out the door to the dumpster. And so Eli didn't.

For a few weeks, it felt like an enormous elephant in the room, clobbering all of their conversations as soon as she tried to open her mouth. But, as it turned out, you could learn to live with an elephant. You could learn how to walk around it without tripping, how to avoid the sensitive trunk, the swishing tail. She hadn't been invited into Anna's room since that afternoon, but today Eli walked in just like always. Anna had thrown out her trophies and taken down her Abby Wambach posters, but she hadn't put anything in their place. Every piece of black clothing she owned was strewn on the floor, covering the rug somewhere underneath, stinking slightly of cigarettes and incense. One boot stuck out from the leg of a skinny jean.

"Anna, it looks like you just moved in and never bothered to unpack," said Eli as she walked by with an armful of dirty clothes. Or maybe, Eli tried not to think, it was more like she was about to leave. There were 341 days until Anna's eighteenth birthday, 388 until graduation. Eli knew her sister kept a tally by her bed. But that was a problem for another day.

"Lucky for you, I'm doing laundry," Anna shouted. "What needs to go in?"

"Are you doing a dark load or a light load? HAHA!"

"You dork. Just give me your clothes."

Anna walked into Eli's room. It was neater than Anna's, but in its own state of in-between-ness. Sam had painted Eli's little room baby-girl pink when he found out that's what the baby would be. Pink walls, pink rug, pink lamp. It was like one of the girls that Eli hated had thrown up all over her room. Eli wasn't a tomboy, or at least not in the way that people thought of tomboys. Eli had never made contact with a ball willingly; she hated the outdoors and couldn't tell the difference between a lug wrench and a screwdriver. Anna had tried to get her to play soccer when they were younger, but all Eli would say was, "I'm not that kind of boy." Eli wasn't any kind of boy, Anna would explain, just her own kind of girl. The world didn't always agree with Anna.

The first time Eli had been called a boy, she was six and she had been wearing a dress. She'd asked a policeman where to find the bathroom, and he'd pointed her to the "little boys' room." There was just something not-girl about her. But there was something not-boy too. It was confusing for everyone, but not for Anna. Eli was Eli. She was soft-hearted, more sensitive than she liked to admit, a good friend and a good sister. Boy or girl had nothing to do with it. Anna looked at her little sister, folding up her too-big jeans, tossing her sports bras in the laundry.

"We should paint your room."

"Oh yeah?" Eli sounded hopeful.

"Yeah, something . . . more you."

"Like rainbow?"

"Very funny, homo. I just mean something a little less . . . aggressively three-year-old girl."

"But Sam painted this."

"It's okay. You're allowed to have a room that's like you."

Eli hadn't so much Come Out as she had just kept being Eli. About a year ago they had been watching TV one Saturday waiting for Mom to come home from the night before, and Eli said, "What do you want to do when you want to kiss someone?

"Kiss them. Who do you want to kiss?"

"Meena."

"She's pretty."

"Isn't she??"

"Oh, Peanut Butter, you've got it bad. Well, the first thing is that you've got to figure out if she likes girls."

"I don't think she does."

"You never know."

"But how do I know if she likes girls? How do I know that even if she likes girls, she likes me?"

"You could tell her how you feel and see what she says."

"That's the worst advice you've ever given me, and when I was four, you told me to put my fork in that socket to see what would happen."

"Look, dude, I'm sorry. You need gaydar; it'll take a while to develop."

"What is gaydar?" Eli moaned. Sometimes it felt like liking girls was way more complicated than it needed to be.

"It's how you tell which girls are into girls or which guys who are into guys. Like radar, but for gays."

"Where do I get that?"

"At the gay store. How would I know?"

"Great."

"You'll figure it out. Have you felt this way about other girls?"

"Well, yeah," said Eli. "I mean, I'm gay."

"Then you better get on top of this gaydar thing."

Eli threw her head into her hands.

"I'm kidding, seester, I'm kidding."

"Straight girl's got jokes," said Eli.

The couch cushion sailed easily from Anna's hands to Eli's head.

"We could paint it white, I guess, maybe yellow? Green?"

"Whatever color you want. Come down to the horrible basement with me and do laundry. Bring your secret bag of quarters—I know you have one." Of course Eli had one. A few hours later, she was folding her clothes and putting them away. After she hung up her favorite hoodie, she started to pick the pink butterfly decal off her closet door.

"Sorry, Sam," she said quietly. "I'm just not that kind of girl." Now that Anna had suggested changing it, all Eli could see was the Pepto-Bismol pink of her room. She peeled off the strawberries and the hearts, the butterflies and the pink stars. She took down the poster of the kitten in the basket with yarn (pink, of course) that had been up since she was born and that she had hardly noticed but now seemed enormous and awful. She rolled up the pink square rug and stuffed it under her bed. Not done, but a good start. She went into Anna's room to see if she would switch her gray comforter for Eli's pink one, but Anna had fallen asleep.

"PB," Anna muttered, still sleeping. "Come." Eli got in and curled up inside the skinny curve of her big sister.

In the morning, it was Eli's turn in the kitchen. Jenny Jakes' Donut Cakes and hot chocolate, what Eli knew how to "cook."

"Thank you for my morning dose of diabetes."

"Anytime," Eli said, between bites of coffee-cake-crumble donut. "I've got a plan for the rest of your day. Eat up."

Eli reached into her back pocket and handed Anna the envelope she'd snagged from Mom's bed. It was from Hoover Middle, and it looked official.

Anna put down her hot chocolate. "What did you do, Eli?"

"I didn't do anything, angry-pants. It's parent-teacher conferences. Tomorrow. Here, I got you a present." Eli tossed her a box of blond hair dye. "There are four more in the bathroom. You better get started if you're going to be Aunt Lisa by tomorrow."

"You owe me, kid."

"I made you breakfast!"

Anna shoved an entire donut into her mouth, flipped Eli off, and headed to the bathroom.

—7—

"KITTY GIRLS, AS Bacchus did unto his maenads, so do I unto you present . . ." Javi announced as he opened up a box of pizza, unloading three Cokes from his backpack. They were sitting in the park near school, waiting for the start of parent-teacher conferences. Eli knew that Javi wasn't an idiot. He had to know that Eli didn't have money; he knew she lived in an apartment, and anyone who lived in an apartment in Middletown was poor. Eli had never once invited Javi to her house or introduced him to her mom. What most people didn't realize about Javi, past the mythology and the RuPaulogy, what his mother's douchebag boyfriend never seemed to bother to notice, was that he was pure love underneath.

He was the kid who would figure that your mother didn't give you money for dinner (he wouldn't know why or where she was, and he wouldn't ask), and so he would show up with pizza and soda like it had fallen from the sky special for the three of you, a love for bacchanalia his likely excuse. Eli wished she could save a slice for Anna, but Anna was busy and it would mess up her perfect, frosted-pink lips. Aunt Lisa would never have a hair out of place, much less pizza grease at the corners of her mouth.

"How was camping with Biff?" Eli asked between bites.

"As awful as you can imagine. We had to tie food up in the trees so the bears wouldn't eat it. Bears!" The three of them shivered in unison as Javi continued, "Bacchus forgive me, but nature is the worst. Scratch that. Biff is the worst. Nature and I can exist separately, at least."

"I would have traded you," said Meena.

"I thought you liked weddings?" Eli asked. She had memorized every fact that Meena had ever revealed about herself. Fact #117: Meena likes weddings. Fact #117b: Only Indian ones, where the bride doesn't wear white.

"I do, but my cousin married this boring banker, and all of his boring banker friends were there, and my other cousin who is totally creepy kept staring at me and saying, 'Wow, Meena, you've really developed,' which is a total child-molester thing to say, a, and, b, he's my *cousin*."

"Foul," said Javi.

"Totally, " added Eli.

"Anyone else worried about conferences tonight?" Javi asked them.

"I'm worried that Mr. Wenzel is going to mention my detentions. It's possible that I told my parents that I've joined a community service club to explain my late arrivals at home."

"Meena! Bold! I would expect that from our little Eli—you know she's more devious than she seems— but not from you!"

"I've got layers of devious that you've never dreamed of," Meena said with a wink and a twirl. "Come on, it's starting."

"Are you nervous, Eli?"

"Huh?"

"Earth to Eli, come in, Eli!"

"Sorry, yeah, guess I am nervous."

"Your mom is so chill, though!"

Mom is super chill, Eli thought. The chillest. Mom is so chill that she hasn't been home in a week because she's at court-mandated rehab and I live with my sister who is pretending to be my aunt. It's all very chill.

Sometimes, Eli thought, when you stop telling the truth, it's impossible to start.

"Yeah, she can't come tonight. Um, she has to work. My Aunt Lisa is coming instead. I've got to go meet her; I'll catch you guys later. Good luck!" Eli took off running for the school. It sucked lying to Meena and Javi, but what choice did she have? Javi's mom was the freaking principal; she couldn't risk her finding out where Mom was. And her life felt so complicated next to Meena's—how could she even begin to explain this to someone whose major family drama usually involved an upset at game night?

She texted Anna to meet her in the bathroom by the cafeteria. They could work out a plan from there without the spying eyes of her wonderful friends, who would of course recognize Anna, blond and prim though she was.

Eli put her feet up on the rim of the toilet and waited. Soon, she was joined by Aunt Lisa, a blur of blond and pastel through the slats of the stall.

"Anna, in here," she whispered. Anna opened the door.

"What is wrong with you, Eli? You're acting like you work for the CIA, which for the record, you'd be really bad at. Feet up on the toilet seat? Oldest trick in the book."

"Sorry, I'm nervous."

"Nothing to be nervous about, little one. Aunt Lisa's here," Anna said, reapplying lip gloss in the mirror. "Let's go."

Mrs. Leger in science was up first. She'd been at the school forever, and it seemed like everyone, even Principal Calderón, was just waiting for her to retire. Anna walked in at 7:01 and out at 7:03. "You're doing just fine, Eliza."

"Ugh, I know. She won't call me Eli, the worst. 'I shall call you by the name your parents chose for you,'" Eli whined, imitating Mrs. Leger's high-pitched nasal drone.

"All the better for us. She taught me five years ago, didn't even blink when she saw me."

"Anna, I'm not sure she'd recognize *me*."

"Who's Anna?"

"Fine, we have to go to my homeroom teacher next."

As they walked in the door of 5-B, Eli tried to keep her cool. Mr. Sposato always seemed to be paying a little more attention than she wished he was. Fortunately, this was only his second year at the school. He had never taught Anna; he didn't even know Eli had a big sister.

"Ms. Reynolds, it's so nice to finally meet you," he said, greeting Anna at the door, the same way he greeted every student before every class. Mr. Sposato was a kid favorite, which was interesting because he taught French, wore dorky ties, and seemingly had no interest in sports. Still, the girls never cut his class, and the boys never threw things at him. During homeroom on Fridays he would remind them, "If you can't love yourself, how in the hell are you going to love somebody else?" which Eli was pretty sure came straight from *Drag Race*. But instead of rolling their eyes, everyone nodded at his profundity. Some girls wiped away a tear when no one was looking. He looked at Anna closely, a question mark floating over "Ms. Reynolds."

"I'm actually Eli's aunt, Lisa," Anna said confidently. "My sister had to work tonight, so she asked me to come in her place." They shook hands, and Anna tried out a slow, wide smile.

"Great! Come on in." Mr. Sposato seemed a little impervious to the wonders of the Anna Smile, but it was just homeroom. Mr. Sposato ushered them both inside. He liked to do conferences with both the parents *and* the kid, probably just to make things as awkward as possible, Eli figured. He explained how homeroom worked, that if there were any problems, he'd be the person parents would be hearing from, and that he hoped he was the person that the kids in his homeroom could turn to if they needed anything. Maybe he was hoping that this invitation would fall on Eli's ears. It didn't. It wasn't like she heard him say that and rolled her eyes thinking, "What could you do for me?" or that she thought, "Please, I've got this under control." She didn't even hear him.

The night had gone off more or less without a hitch except for Eli's history teacher, Ms. Matheson, who'd had Anna in eighth grade and who kept exclaiming about the family resemblance.

"My, but you look just like Anna! And you can't be a whit older than her!"

"Sweet of you to say," Anna said, her voice dropping an octave as she tried to sound older. "But I'm actually twenty-three. Good genes, I guess!"

"I'll say!"

The girls blushed and thanked her and got out of that room as quickly as possible, while Anna mumbled something about being Mom's *younger* sister.

"Close," Eli exhaled as they turned down the hallway.

"Too close. I've got to hang up Aunt Lisa after tonight." She laughed as they turned the corner. Suddenly her voice changed. "Walk fast," she said quietly, through gritted teeth and pink lips.

"What?" Eli said too loudly. Anna put her hand on Eli's shoulder, hard, and pushed. "Don't push me!"

"Hello there, Eliza." Mr. Peterson seemed to come out of nowhere.

"Uh, hi." Eli had never had him; she didn't take shop or play soccer.

"Gosh, you look so familiar, and yet, I don't think we've met." He was standing right in front of Anna now, blocking their path. One thick hand extended to shake hers.

"I'm Lisa Reynolds, Eli's aunt. It's nice to meet you."

"Well, isn't Anna just your spitting image."

"I suppose."

"What a lucky, lucky girl." Mr. Peterson was the soccer coach for the middle and high school teams. He had black hair and blue eyes, and all the girls always loved him, until they eventually quit the team like Anna had.

"Yup, and I'm their lucky aunt. It's nice to meet you. We've got to get going. Long day."

Mr. Peterson moved to one side to let them pass, making it so Anna brushed against him as she walked by.

"Please tell Anna I say hello. We miss her on the field."

When they got out to the car, Anna's hands were shaking.

"Open the door," Eli shouted from the other side of the car.

"Just give me a goddamn minute, Eli." Anna turned around, leaning her back against the car door. "Damn it," she said sadly, angrily, as she clutched the keys in her trembling hand. Eli came around to her side.

"What happened? What's wrong?"

"Nothing. I'm fine. Let's go home."

"That is obviously not true."

"Leave it alone, Eli. I just want to go home."

They rode home in silence. They walked into the quiet apartment, and Eli turned on the lights in the kitchen.

"I'm making hot chocolate," she said. "And then you're going to tell me what's going on."

Anna didn't say anything, but she sat down at the kitchen table, which Eli took as a good sign. She put hot mugs in front of each of them, three-fourths marshmallows, one-fourth chocolate. Anna smiled in spite of herself. Eli was putting it all together—the black clothes, the constant snarl, the soccer trophies in the trash.

"What did he do to you?" Eli asked.

"Nothing."

"Don't bullshit me, Anna."

"He didn't do anything to me. He's just a creep. And he was a creep the entire time I was on his team. The same way he was tonight. Nothing you can complain about, you know? Nothing that if you told another person, they'd be able to do anything or make it stop. Just this side of okay. Just this side of only in your head."

"Like how he made you walk past him tonight so he could casually brush up against you?"

"You saw that?"

"I did. I wanted to puke."

"Yeah. Like that. Like that all the time. And other shit too, patting your ass when you come off the field, like that's normal, like it's all just part of the game. His hands on your shoulders, like, all the time for no reason. Telling you that you might need a new uniform soon, that yours is looking tight. He's an asshole."

"Is that why you quit?"

Anna sighed. "I quit because he started offering me rides after practice, saying he knew Mom wasn't home, that she hadn't made any games yet this season. And when I said no, he stopped playing me. Just like that. He wouldn't look at me, wouldn't make me captain even though the whole team voted for me, wouldn't let me start, and then wouldn't let me play at all."

"Why didn't you . . ." Eli fell quiet. She could answer her own question. "Who would you tell?"

"Exactly. And what would I tell them? He said I needed a new uniform? That's not a crime. I'm not captain of my team? Also not a crime. He sees I don't have a ride and so he offers me one? Oooh, call the cops."

"You're probably not the only one. I bet he does that to other girls too."

"Eli," Anna said, low and slow. "You can't tell anyone."

"I know."

They slept in Anna's bed that night, Anna facing the wall, and Eli curled around her for once. Just before they fell asleep, Eli said, "Can I tell you something terrible?"

"Uh-huh."

"Like really, really terrible?"

"Mmm-hmm," said Anna, trying to keep her eyes open.

"It's easier without Mom."

And then they slept.

8

BOTH GIRLS WOKE up early the following Saturday. Anna made pancakes while Eli dressed and redressed. A button-down? Was that too Boy Scout? A hoodie didn't seem to acknowledge the occasion. She decided to go with her favorite jeans and what she called her baseball shirt—white middle and red sleeves.

"You look cute, Eli. You know your cuteness isn't going to keep her sober."

"Shut up and give me my pancakes."

They ate in nervous silence. Anna looked like she always did, dunked in black ink, drinking coffee (black, of course).

"Is it far to Green Hills?" Eli asked.

"Thirty-nine minutes."

"Why couldn't she have stayed around here? Should we bring her something?"

"Like what?" Both girls looked around the kitchen. Eli's purple flowers had long since died, and there was a half-empty box of donuts on the counter and the leftovers from the chili that Anna had made on Wednesday in the fridge.

"I guess not."

It was hard to believe Mom had been gone for three weeks. They sang along to the radio the whole way there, better than talking, especially since there was nothing to say. Eli knew Anna didn't want to hear her secret hopes that it would work, that Mom would greet them clear-eyed and happy, fun and funny like she could be sometimes.

Mom wasn't only this Mom. She was also the Mom who picked Eli up from school after a bad week during those long months before she had Meena and Javi and the world seemed made out of Kevins. Eli had come home with spit in her hair. Mom cleaned her up, taught her how to throw a punch (though Eli still hadn't done it), and the next day a few minutes before the lunch bell rang, Eli was called to the office. Mom was waiting there. "Eli, did you forget about your dentist appointment?" Mom was saying in a sugary Mom-voice not her own.

"What?"

"Kids, right?" Mom said to the attendance secretary.

"My son always forgets," she offered.

"Well, we don't want to be late, knucklehead." And she threw her arm over Eli's shoulder and led her out of the school. Pulling out of the parking lot, Mom took a right instead of a left.

"Mom, the dentist isn't this way."

"That's why we're not going to the dentist." First they went to the diner, where Eli got to order whatever she wanted (a hamburger and French fries, a root beer float) and then they went to the movies. It was *that* Mom Eli hoped was waiting for her behind the doors of Green Hills. Confident, happy, armed with a plan.

Eli knew Anna didn't want to hear those Mom stories, though she knew Anna had to have plenty of them too—Mom teaching her how to do her eyeliner, both girls sitting with their arms wrapped around their knees watching Mom get dressed to go out for the night. Dance parties in the kitchen. Mom and Sam kissing under mistletoe. Anna gripped the steering wheel tighter. Eli knew that instead Anna would think about the red and blue lights shining on their bedroom walls. The particular sound of a cop knock that they both wished they didn't recognize. That time that Mom thought Anna's room was the bathroom, and she woke up to Mom puking on her desk, right on her math homework. The time she scored the winning goal at the state championships, the ones that Anna'd begged Mom to come to, the ones that Mom swore she wouldn't miss for anything, and then did. Mom coming in at 7:00 A.M. while Sam was making breakfast for both girls. Eli knew that was the only Mom that Anna would want to talk to her about. That other Mom was just a ghost, Anna would say. And only fools believed in those. Eli slumped down in her seat.

They made the long walk from the parking lot to a large brick building that was neither green nor surrounded by hills. The chill of the air conditioner took the girls by surprise when they walked through the automatic doors. Anna zipped up her hoodie. Eli rubbed her arms.

"Can I help you?" asked an official-looking woman behind the front desk.

"We're here to see Carrie Reynolds."

"Family Day. Seventh floor. Take the elevator at the end of the hall to the seventh floor and check in at the front desk. You'll have to leave your belongings there." They looked at each other. They had no belongings.

On the seventh floor, the man behind the desk put checks by their names and gave them name tags, and asked each of them three times if they had any contraband on them, including hand sanitizer or e-cigarettes, before showing them to the conference room. There was a man and his new baby; a woman and her two teenage sons in backwards lacrosse caps who shared the same bored face; an elderly man and woman with similar short gray haircuts, wide hips, and big bellies; and a tall woman with very short hair nervously fiddling with her wedding ring.

"I'm Cliff. I'll be leading our opening session today," said the man at the front of the room. Cliff was short and thick, bald and muscular. "So, here's a question: Why are we here? To help your loved ones? You've already done everything you can. Why should this be different? They're the same people they were before they arrived at Green Hills, aren't they?" A few of the mothers in the room nodded their heads. Anna crossed her arms.

"I remember sitting in a cafeteria waiting for my family coming to see me at a rehab just like this one. I remember thinking that I wasn't sure that it would be any different. I also remember thinking that I must be a total monster, because here they were, my family coming to Family Day at a rehab, again, to visit me, again, to hope for me, again, to wait for me to disappoint them, again. It was my fourteenth time in rehab. I was twenty-five years old. I didn't think I had a disease, unless being an asshole was a disease."

A smirk danced in the corner of Anna's mouth.

"The thing is, it's hard being an asshole. It really makes you want to drink. Who wants to spend their life letting down their families? Who wants to throw up in their boss's office at nine in the morning? Who wants to be that guy at your party? An asshole. And assholes need to drink. It was somewhere around week two of my fourteenth rehab that I started to understand that it wasn't about being an asshole. It wasn't about choice. In fact, as much as I liked to feel like a big, powerful dude (okay, a small, powerful dude), when it came to booze, I'd lost any choice I'd ever had somewhere between eighth and ninth grade. I was a shy kid, short and scrawny—the two of you could've taken my lunch money just by asking for it," he said, pointing at the lacrosse boys.

"I couldn't talk to girls, I couldn't dance, I couldn't play ball, I couldn't look you in the eye. And I couldn't stand myself. Every single day, it felt like I'd gotten to school just after the meeting where they told everyone what to do, how to act, how to make friends, and I'd missed it.

"That summer, my big brother threw a party while our parents were away. Me and one of my dork friends walked around sneaking the drinks away from the unsuspecting teenagers. Before I knew it, my cheeks were warm, my body felt a million miles away, and I finally knew peace. Thirteen years old, and I'd never had a minute of quiet in my brain. Alcohol did that for me. It also let me go up to the prettiest girl there, and just start a conversation. I think I even danced. I looked at my dork friend and thought, why do I spend time with this loser? I'd discovered the secret to happiness, confidence, and quieting down the squirrel nest of my brain. That night I kissed my first girl, I fought with my friend, I blacked out, I threw up, and woke up with a thirteen-year-old's hangover.

"That night was exactly like every single night I'd have for the next twelve years. Get drunk, kiss a girl, fight with a friend, black out, throw up, wake up hungover. I lost friends, my scholarship, jobs, the trust of my friends and family, and my self-respect. And I kept at it, night after night. So, here's the thing. I'm not an idiot. And I'm not an asshole. So, why? I was chasing that feeling I got that first night—the relief, the million miles to my brain, the confidence, the quiet. But it wasn't ever there, not like that, even though I spent a lot of my time, and money, and life, looking for it. I'm an alcoholic. I have a disease that loves alcohol way more than it loves anything else, including me. It wants more, more, more, and it's willing to arrange my entire life around getting more. Nothing is more important, even the things that are more important to *me*. When I was drinking, I didn't love any of those people waiting for me in a room just like this as much as I loved alcohol. I wouldn't have said it, I didn't think it was true, but alcohol did something for me that they never could."

"Oh my god, what's your point?" said one of the lacrosse boys.

Cliff grinned, liked he'd been waiting for exactly this moment. "This: whoever brought you here today, this is the shit that brought *them* here. They've got a lot to learn, but so do you. The chance of them surviving outside of here goes up significantly if you know the difference between assholeism and alcoholism.

"I'm not saying you need to forgive your loved one. They've treated you like crap; you have a rolling list of the games, graduations, birthdays, weddings, funerals, Christmases that they've missed or ruined. The money, the late-night calls, the emergency rooms, the close acquaintance with law enforcement. You hate yourself for hanging on to the last shred of love for them, since they only use it to disappoint you. You try to turn your heart to stone, and that weasel just turns right back into muscle on you.

"We're going to deal with all of that. It's going to take time, and your loved ones are going to have to work really hard to earn back even a quarter-smile from you. That's their job. Your job is to get educated about what this disease is and isn't. This is your first Family Day. There will be one each month that your family member is here, and we recommend that in between you attend at least four Al-Anon or Alateen meetings. Go ahead, roll your eyes—I know my big brother did too—but this is a family disease, like it or not, and your loved one isn't the only one who needs to get better."

Mom saw them before they saw her. When Eli and Anna turned the corner into the cafeteria, she ran up from her table and threw her arms around her girls.

"My girls," she said. "My babies." She smelled the same, basically. Maybe a little more like industrial soap and laundry detergent, but still, the same unnameable, untraceable smell of Mom. Eli breathed in.

"We're okay, Mom," said Eli.

"Come sit," she said, holding both their hands. She looked the same too, a little tired, her green eyes bloodshot, but wide open. She was sweating just a little. Her brown hair was up in a ponytail, and she was wearing a gray hoodie and sweatpants, like a uniform. She stared at them expectantly, her hands fluttering up to their faces and then back down to her sides as Anna hissed quietly, "Don't."

Mom opened her mouth to speak; Anna looked away. Eli's eyes bounced between the two of them, the floor, the ceiling. "Thank you both for coming," Mom squeaked out, trying to keep the tears out of her voice, the same ones that were threatening her eyelashes.

Eli managed a smile, managed to look her right in the face for just a second before she had to look away. Had anything ever been this awkward? Thankfully, a boring-looking woman approached the mic at the front of the cafeteria, a boring-looking PowerPoint on display to her side. There were twenty-five minutes of facts about the impact of addiction on the family system. Is that what they were? A system? Maybe a broken one. Then, they moved into individual family sessions with the counselors.

Cliff's office wasn't much, a few chairs and a desk and a computer, white walls with nothing on them. Piles of books, spilling off the shelves onto the floor. Recovery books, sure, but also *Anna Karenina*, *Notes from Underground*, *The Brothers Karamazov*. Eli eyed the spines.

"I flunked out of my Russian Lit class in college," Cliff said. "Trying to make up for lost time. You've probably read all of them, haven't you? Your mom says you're a big reader."

"I'm thirteen. I haven't done a lot of Dostoevsky," Eli said with a small smile.

"Just a little, huh? The minor works?"

Eli laughed. There was something about Cliff that made you want to laugh at his jokes, even if they weren't that funny.

"I'm glad you could make the trip," Cliff said to both girls.

"I am too," said Mom, realizing that they were all waiting for her to talk.

"Go ahead, Carrie," said Cliff quietly.

"I want to tell you a little about what's been going on here. It hasn't been easy." Mom stared at the chipped, pink polish on her fingernails. She had her sleeves pulled down over her hands like a cold, scared little kid. "The first week was really hard; it was mostly just detox. But since then, I've been doing better. Every morning there's group therapy, then I have an individual session with Cliff, then there's a little free time in the afternoon for working out or whatever, and then we go to a meeting at night."

Anna stared out the window.

"Can you tell the girls why you're telling them this?"

"I want you to know that I'm taking this seriously. I know how bad I've screwed up, girls. I know that I've been screwing up for years. But I want to do better. I want to come home. I want home to be a place you like being. Eli, I want to bother you about your homework. Anna, I want to go to your soccer games."

Eli inhaled sharply as Anna snapped to angry attention.

"I quit soccer six months ago." Anna turned to Cliff. "Is she cured yet?"

Eli watched Mom's face try not to crumble. Cliff took a breath and then smiled and waited; Anna wasn't done. "You said it's a disease, fine. Is she cured?"

"You don't get cured. I wish you did. But I've been sober for more than half my life, and still, if I drank a beer tomorrow, I'd be totally shit out of luck."

"Sucks to be you."

Cliff laughed; he seemed genuinely amused. "It's okay. I know how to stay away from that beer. Your mom is learning how to do that too. It's going to take some time though."

Anna crossed her arms and looked at the floor. That wasn't the only thing that was going to take time.

"Look, guys, this whole thing sucks," Cliff said. "It's going to take time for you all to fix your family. In the meantime, be as angry as you need to be. Your mom is doing what she can to get out of here and go home and be able to be a mom to you."

Anna sucked her teeth. Eli looked at her hands.

"I don't have a lot of practice at that," said Mom. "But I'm trying to learn. I miss you both so much." The tears finally won and pushed their way down her face.

"What do you miss about us?" asked Anna angrily. "What do you even know about us? You still think Eli is eight; you think I play soccer. What's Eli's favorite food? Who are her best friends? Do I want to go to college? Can you even answer any of that? Please don't say you miss us. Say you wish you weren't in here—that you'd rather be home. Say, even, that you wish you hadn't hopelessly fucked up our lives. But please don't say you miss us. You don't know anything about us."

"I really wish I hadn't fucked up your lives," said Mom quietly. "And I know that Eli bites her lip when she gets nervous, and that you're very busy chasing trouble, and that even though you both worry about me, I worry about you too. And Anna, if you think that I'll forgive myself for leaving you to raise Eli, you're wrong. And if you think I'll ever forgive myself for not being the mother to you that you are to Eli, you're wrong about that too."

"Can we stop talking about me like I'm not here, and like I'm a baby?" said Eli.

"Good idea. Let's just stop talking," Anna growled.

"This is probably enough for today," said Cliff. "You should both think about attending some Alateen meetings before our next session. It will help."

Both girls looked at the floor.

"Any questions?" Cliff looked at Eli and Anna.

"Yeah. Where's the rent money?" Anna asked Mom.

Mom looked up, surprised.

"Rent, Mom? We don't all live in a bubble of inspirational posters and prayer. Next week is the first. Where's the rent money?"

Mom swallowed.

"Does Chuck have it?" Chuck was Mom's boss at the construction company where she'd been a secretary for the last five years.

"Chuck . . ."

"I can go by the office and pick it up," Anna offered.

"Carrie, rigorous honesty," Cliff said. "You need to tell them."

"Chuck fired me two months ago."

Anna stared at her, lips slightly apart. She blinked once, very slowly. She shook her head from one side to the next before she stood up. Eli held her breath, waiting for the explosion she knew was coming.

"Fuck this. Eli, I'm done. Meet me in the car when you are." The blue metal door closed hard behind her.

"I'm so sorry, Eli," Mom said.

"Mom, honestly, I love you and I know how hard you're working but please, please, please, stop saying you're sorry."

"Well said," said Cliff, tossing a soft smile to Eli and a stern look to Mom. Mom nodded to herself.

"Okay."

"I think this is enough for today. Carrie, why don't you walk Eli out?"

At the door, Cliff stopped Eli with a hand on her shoulder. "You should think about Alateen. Here's the listing for the meetings in Middletown." She stuffed it in her pocket. "Don't worry," he said with a quiet chuckle. "You don't have to thank me."

"I won't, then," Eli said, grinning just a little.

"Bye, kid."

Mom was a puddle of tears. She cried and hugged Eli more than Eli wanted to be hugged. She was holding Eli tight for the fourth time when a woman in floral scrubs whispered in Mom's ear, and she pulled back.

"I love you, Eli, in my own useless way. I really do."

"I know you do." And then the whoosh of the automatic doors carried Eli to the car.

9

AT LUNCH ON MONDAY, Meena slid Eli something that looked vaguely like a cookie. "My newest recipe. They're gluten-free, sugar-free, dairy-free, and nut-free. I made them for my sister, but I had a few left over." Meena's sister was allergic to *everything*.

"What *do* they have in them? Dirt?" Javi rolled his eyes. Eli took a bite, and a big swallow of milk.

"They're really good, just, um, a little dry." They all laughed as Eli choked down the rest of the cookie.

"You are a better friend than I am," Javi said, patting her on the back. "Who's in for *Rocky Horror* this weekend? They're showing it at the Criterion at midnight on Friday. Mom and Douchebag have a date. They won't notice if I'm not home. They'll be relieved."

"There's no way in hell my parents will let me go," said Meena.

"They can come too; your parents are down for a good time," suggested Javi.

"Yeah, thanks, no. I'd rather not have those particular images burned into my psyche forever."

"I can go," said Eli.

"Really? Your mom won't mind?"

"She really won't."

"Your mom is so cool," Meena said, jealous.

Friday night, Eli walked through Javi's living room, trying not to notice how out of place her dirty sneakers felt on the plush carpet, trying not to accidentally bump into the sparkly, new, and impossibly fragile things that his mother had on every surface. Once she was safely inside Javi's room, she exhaled, throwing herself into his overstuffed armchair, swinging her legs over the side.

"So, who are you going as?" Eli asked. Javi, Meena, and Eli had watched *Rocky Horror* countless times in this very room with bowls of gourmet popcorn and dreams of going to a screening.

"In my dreams, Rocky. In my thirteen-year-old, still-have-my-baby-fat reality, I'm going as Dr. Frank-N-Furter in the surgical gown. I figure I can use one of my mother's boring gray dresses and her pearls. And all my parts will be covered."

"If you fluff up those curls, you'll have a proper Frank-N-Furter crown. Could be your lucky night. What are we going to do with me? I'm not exactly a Janet."

"We both know who you are," Javi said.

Eli blushed. Javi brought Eli into his mother's room.

"This is too weird, Javi. I know she's your mom, but she's also my principal and I don't really want to know what her bedroom looks like."

"Get over it. We're here on a mission." He started digging through the space in his mom's closet reserved for Douchebag's clothes.

"Are you sure he won't mind?"

"Eli, this man has nothing but copies of the same shirts, same shoes, same everything. He won't mind; he won't notice. But first we've got to take care of those tetas."

Eli looked down at her chest. "What can we do? I'm already wearing a sports bra. Honestly, I'm already wearing two."

"That's why god made duct tape. Take off your shirt." Eli stood in the middle of Javi's mother's bedroom, by the white desk and mirror that Javi called a vanity, and watched as Javi wound duct tape around her sports bras. When he was done, he tossed her one of his undershirts to put on under the Douchebag's white button-down.

"There," Javi said, parting Eli's hair on the side. "Dork transformation complete."

"Right, because dork is such a stretch for me." Still, looking in the mirror made Eli smile in a way she didn't know how to describe. She looked like Brad from the movie. Sure, she was wearing the Douchebag's terrible brown shoes and khaki jacket zipped halfway up, and she would never wear her hair in Brad's comb-over in real life, but she also looked undeniably like herself. And she loved the feeling of her boobs strapped down to her chest, loved the familiar flatness that she'd lost in the last year or two.

Javi and Eli took a selfie to send to Meena. His curls framed his face, pearls on full display. Eli tried to make her most confident Brad face, unable to keep herself from thinking that maybe Meena would like her better like this, in boy drag that wasn't really so much like drag. Meena sent back a kissy face, a fire, and a sad face. She hoped that the kiss was for her. Or maybe the fire. Maybe Meena thought Brad was hot. She looked at Javi, all curls and eye shadow and confidence, and shook her head. Confidence is what makes a fire, and she had none at all.

They must have looked crazy riding their bikes down the identical (house, shrubs, house, shrubs, stop sign) streets of Laurel Crest. Past the lawns, all clipped to the exact same millimeter, the pools glistening in the moonlight, the garages built for three cars. Javi was making the most of riding his bike in his mom's heels. Eli was doing the best she could to keep the sock in her pants from falling out as she followed him, her comb-over rustling in the night breeze.

When they got to the theater, Javi flashed his phone at the ticket-taker as Eli reached in her pocket for the crumpled twenty she'd grabbed from her stash on the way out the door. "Oh, there was a two-for-one deal, Eli, I got it," he said quickly as he ushered her through the door.

Was there a word for being grateful, relieved, and annoyed at once? She didn't want Javi thinking she was some charity case that he had to look out for. She also didn't want to spend the money if she didn't have to. The second they sat down in the theater, surrounded by fellow freaks—men in maids' uniforms, red feather boas, or tiny gold shorts; women with their hair dyed every imaginable color, wearing wedding dresses or doctor's coats—Javi's assessment of her money issues was the last thing on her mind. She couldn't stop staring and she couldn't stop smiling.

"Oh my god, stop, you look like such a virgin."

"Shut up, you know I just haven't found the right person."

"Eli, Jesus, I mean a *Rocky Horror* virgin, someone who hasn't seen it in the theater before."

"So? So are you!" With that, the lights went down and unlike every other theater she'd ever been in, this one got louder and louder as the show began. Suddenly, a perfect Frank-N-Furter appeared on stage, lips bright red in a vicious grin.

"All right, where are our virgins?" The lights went back up. All the eyes in their row turned to Javi and Eli. "Virgins! Virgins! Virgins!" they chanted.

"Get your asses up there, babies," said a man in a maid outfit next to them.

"Told you so," whispered Javi. Javi, Eli, and a few other (un)fortunate souls headed to the front of the auditorium.

"Oooh, fresh meat," said Frank-N-Furter, running a gloved hand under Eli's chin and draping it over Javi's shoulder. "And jailbait at that." Down the line Frank-N-Furter went, painting red *V*s on each of their cheeks with his blood-red lipstick.

"You'll all keep your eyes on these virgins, won't you?"

"Yes, ma'am!" replied the audience.

Back in their seats, Javi whispered, teasing, "Don't worry, you can't even see the *V*, you're so red."

They sang along to every word, throwing rice during the wedding scene, ducking the spray from the water guns during the thunderstorm scene. During "The Time Warp," everyone filed out to the aisles to take a jump to the left and a step to the right. As they swiveled their hips, Eli-as-Brad noticed someone (a boy? A girl? She couldn't tell . . .) dressed as Columbia, gold hat, pink bustier, gold jacket and tiny gold shorts, fishnets, short red hair, and a wicked grin. Columbia winked at Eli-as-Brad. Eli lost track of whether it was time to jump to the left or step to the right or how to breathe. Columbia walked over to her.

"Careful there, virgin." Columbia reached for Eli's elbow.

"Thanks."

"You are something, aren't you?"

"Huh?"

"Oooh, and you don't even know it." Columbia leaned in close to Eli's ear. "We're all going to fall in love with you. Just you wait." She (?) kissed Eli's cheek, right on her *V*.

Eli felt herself blush all over. She breathed in, inhaling Columbia's perfume. She felt her stomach flip.

"Go get 'em." Columbia swatted Eli's butt playfully and made her way over to her seat at the other end of the theater. Eli watched her long legs walk away. She breathed in. Cinnamon.

"Eli, sit down." Javi was pulling her back into her seat.

"Javi, this is the weirdest night of my life."

"But also the best, am I right?"

"Absolutely."

10

ELI AND ANNA both slept until noon, finally meeting in the kitchen in their different degrees of blissful mess. Eli looked up from her cereal and stared at her sister.

"Oh my god, what did you do last night?"

"A lady never tells."

"And you're no lady, so spill!" A coy smile was Anna's only response. "You got with the Jacket?? I'm happy for you, sister. High five."

"Thanks," said Anna, taking a breath.

"What's wrong?" asked Eli.

"Well, it's Saturday, PB. It's Saturday, and the day after tomorrow's Monday, and that means that we need to come up with rent and we don't have it." Anna's words were true, but the glow from the night before made it seem as if they were talking about some other thirteen- and seventeen-year-olds who were totally screwed.

"I hear the words you're saying . . ."

"What did you do last night? Did you finally make out with Meena or something?"

"Nah. Turns out the world's just a lot bigger than I thought, that's all."

"Okay, Eli the Cryptic. Don't tell me. But come back to Earth; we've got to figure this out, even if the world is big, even if it does have Jason in it."

"How much do we need?"

"Eight hundred and ninety-five dollars."

"For all this, huh?" It'd been a while since their cleaning extravaganza. "What do we have left of the nine-sixty?"

"We still have a lot of it." Anna reached for the envelope they kept on top of the fridge. "Looks like . . ." Anna frowned. "Oh. Well, we have six hundred and fifty left."

"How is that possible?"

"Gas, feeding you."

"Feeding you too."

"Yeah, so, gas, food, the twenty that was there before you went to Javi's but isn't there now. It adds up, you know."

"I guess I'm just supposed to be a nun who sits home and waits for you. But, here, I didn't spend it."

"I'm not saying that. I'm saying we have six-fifty—sorry, six-seventy—we owe a grand, and we have to figure out how to eat food and put gas in the car for the next two months. That's all."

"Feels real now, huh?" Eli said, leaning back in her chair.

"Yup. It feels like, Jason who?"

"Jason who, except you still blush when you say it." Eli smiled. "Maybe Kyle would take half?"

"Our asshole landlord? Have you met him?"

"Yes."

"And your conclusion is that he'd take half?"

"What else can we do?"

"I honestly have no idea."

Eli brought Anna into Mom's room. She gestured to the pile of mail on the bed.

"Maybe Mom gets unemployment?"

The pile had grown to take up most of one side of the bed. They sat on opposite sides and started to tear through envelopes.

"Well, this is depressing," said Eli, after a few minutes.

"What?"

"Bills on bills on bills. We have even less money than we think we do."

"We're not paying Mom's bills. They're not going to cut off the lights. Not yet, anyway. This one says second notice. We'll wait for the third. And who cares about the rest? Sorry about your credit card bill, Mom."

Eli came across an envelope marked "LR" in the corner. She tucked it into her back pocket while Anna tore open another letter.

"Sweet," she said.

"What? Unemployment?"

"Yup. Five fifty. We're safe," it looked like she was going to smile, but she didn't. "There's the little matter of, you know, eating, not getting the lights turned off, but hey, at least this palace is ours for another month. We'll figure out the rest."

Anna threw on her jacket and came back twenty minutes later with a grin and a fistful of bills.

"Peter?"

"Peter is the greatest. Man, he misses Mom bad." Peter ran the corner store and always seemed to have a crush on Mom. He was happy to help out her girls and cash the check for them. The girls sat together on the stoop watching the sun go down over Middletown, down over the weekend and the pile of mail. The evening would be spent looking for change in the couch, old birthday cards, and all of Mom's purses. They made it this time. But then Tuesday would come. And then what?

Monday came, as it always did. And Eli and Javi did "The Time Warp" for Meena.

"A drag queen kissed Eli!" Javi shouted to Meena as they lay outside under their tree after school.

"That is not what happened," Eli said through a half smile.

"That is entirely what happened! A guy dressed as a girl kissed Eli. What about my sentence was false?"

"The kiss part? It was a peck on the cheek."

"And a slap on the ass."

"Whatever, it was nothing."

"That's not what your face said."

"Of course she kissed you," said Meena, laughing. "I mean, Eli, you make a very cute Brad."

Eli's stomach flipped. Cutecutecute. Very cute. They didn't talk about the way it felt to be on the bikes, watching Javi's high heels pushing against the pedals just ahead of her. The freedom of riding through his neighborhood together in full drag. Maybe there weren't words for that.

"Ugh, that's my mom," Javi said, looking at his phone. "Valete, puellae. I've got to go."

Meena and Eli lay under the tree together, looking up through its branches to the blue sky.

"So, did you like the kiss?" asked Meena, not looking at her.

Eli could do this. She would answer. She would talk to Meena about kissing girls, or people who looked like girls. Suddenly, Mr. Peterson's face appeared between the branches and blue sky, looking over her spread out on the grass.

"Eliza, could I have a moment?"

"Her name's Eli," Meena called as Eli got to her feet. Mr. Peterson put his arm around her shoulders and walked her a few feet away.

"How's your sister?"

"She's fine," Eli said, trying to keep her voice neutral when what she wanted to say was, Don't ever ask, don't ever mention, don't ever think about my sister again.

"Well, you tell her it was nice to see her the other day."

Eli could feel her pulse racing, the faint sound of static in her ears.

"You mean my aunt?"

"I mean your sister, kid. I don't know who you two think you're fooling with that. But I would recognize our Anna anywhere."

Eli said nothing.

"So, where is your mother? Why wasn't she here? Off on a bender again?"

Eli turned red.

"You can't be surprised that I know, Eliza. This is a small town. She drinks at the bar by my house. Every night, except for the last month or so. She on the wagon?"

Eli's heart was beating out of her chest. She only caught every fourth word or so.

"I didn't think so. But she's not home, is she? Because she hasn't been at the bar, and that woman would be at the bar, you know? Of course you do. I didn't think much of it, until I saw Anna here the other night in that ludicrous 'disguise.' You tell your sister to come down here, and she and I can talk about it like adults, since that's so clearly what she thinks she is. Of course, if I don't get to talk to her, I'll have to turn things over to Principal Calderón. Can't have two minors on their own; that just wouldn't be right."

He dropped his arm, turned away, and walked to his car as if Eli was just one more chore he had to do after school, one more mark off his to-do list. She watched him go, her eyes wide, hoping that if she held them as open as possible she wouldn't cry, wouldn't crumble.

"What did that sleazebag want?" asked Meena, suddenly by her side.

"Nothing," Eli said.

"You know, you don't have to be so mysterious all the time, Eli. You can talk to me."

Eli said nothing because there was nothing to say. Where would the story even start? Besides, she *couldn't* tell Meena and Javi any of this, not with Principal Calderón sitting at Javi's dinner table every night. Eli gave Meena a hug and walked all the way home.

—11—

ELI LIKED PLANS, and that Friday, she woke up with one. She got on the bus with a humming in her chest, a plan flapping its wings against her ribcage. Eli had always been a Grade A snoop. It had gotten her in endless amounts of trouble when she was younger and not as slick as she prided herself on being now. She had gotten caught with her hand in someone else's cubby in kindergarten, with Anna's journal under her pillow in second grade and again in fourth.

She'd had a copy of the master key for months. She wasn't sure why she'd done it, why that small silver key seemed to call her name way back in October. Maybe she just wanted to see if she could. Was she really so invisible that she could take the key from the secretary's desk, get a copy made at lunch, and bring it back without ever having to face a chorus of young-lady-what-do-you-think-you're-doings? She was exactly that invisible. She wasn't sure why she'd wanted the key so badly when she'd taken it. But today she knew what it had always been meant for.

In English, she watched the clock, wondering if Mr. Peterson had seen it yet. Had he opened his grade book for his first period class? Had he seen the paper she'd slipped in among his carefully alphabetized pages of names? A picture of the Crypt Keeper, the worst one she could find, maggots in his eyes, skin worn away to bone, and at the top in bold letters, "Would you want him touching you?" and then, "We don't want you touching us." She'd made three more, one for each of his classes for the day so that he'd see them as he took roll. She wanted to imagine his face. Did he go red? Pale? Did he start to sweat? Lose his train of thought? Did the class ask if he was okay? Did he ignore it and throw it away? What about the second time he saw it? The third?

Sitting on the bleachers with Meena and Javi, Eli barely ate her sandwich.

"What's up, Eli? Not hungry?" asked Javi.

"Oh, I'm just out of it."

"You've been saying that a lot lately."

"Yeah, but today it's a good thing. Today's a good day."

Javi and Meena exchanged confused glances and went back to their discussion of the salient moments of *Grey's Anatomy;* they'd been working their way through all sixteen seasons together. Today's topic was a continuation of their ongoing McDreamy versus McSteamy battle. Javi also delivered a eulogy memorializing the breakup of Calzona and their sapphic love. No spoilers were allowed and no internet permitted while they took bets on which characters the show would kill off first. Eli laughed at their jokes, mostly because it gave her a reason to let out the smile she'd been holding in all morning.

During math, Eli asked to go to the bathroom. She had the thirteen other copies tucked between her too-big hoodie and her T-shirt. As she knew they would have, the soccer girls had lined up their bags by the locker room. Checking over her shoulder each time, she quickly slipped one piece of paper into every bag and went back to math.

At game time, Eli hid in the pink locker room, feet up on the toilet, floating over the pink and white tiles. She didn't care what Anna had said; this was a tried-and-true method of spying. Each girl grabbed her bag on the way in, tossing it onto the floor. They lined up the way eighth grade girls always did, by popularity, the tallest ones with the biggest boobs leading the way, followed by their pack of still-developing lemmings. She could hear Charmaine's voice going a million miles a minute with Tiffany. Hillary came in next laughing with—was it Danae? Voices getting louder as each girl opened her bag to take out her uniform. Speckles of silence as they noticed the pieces of paper at the bottom. "What is this?" Embarrassed giggles.

"Hillary, did you see this?" cried an underling.

"See what?"

"This!"

"Where did you get that?"

"It was in my bag."

"Mine too."

A cacophony of mine-toos. Charmaine and Tiffany were still talking at full volume, oblivious.

"Hey Charmaine," said Hillary, tentatively, always respectful and a little fearful of her captain. "Charmaine!"

"What?" Charmaine's voice bit at Hillary. She hated to be interrupted, particularly while holding court in her queendom.

"Did you see this?"

"What is *this*?"

"There's probably one in your bag too. Check. There's one in each of ours." The moment Eli had been waiting for. She wanted to take a deep breath; she wanted to laugh or cry. She sat stiller than she'd ever been in her life.

"'Has Peterson put his hands on you? A game is no excuse for an ass-grab. #keepyourhandsoffme.'"

"Mine says, 'Peterson's not brushing up against you because it's crowded. #keepyourhandsoffme.'"

"Mine says, 'Tell him no. Being a coach doesn't give him a right to your body. #keepyourhandsoffme.'"

"Who the hell made these?"

Silence.

Hillary said, "Well, this is total bullshit. I'm sorry, but this is the work of a loser virgin with time on her hands. Peterson is just Peterson. If you can't take it, get off the team."

"Shut up, Hillary." That was Charmaine.

"What?"

"I said, shut up."

Charmaine didn't say anything else. Everyone got dressed in silence.

Eli waited for the sound of an empty locker room. She put her feet down one at a time, letting the pins and needles wave over her legs. She smiled to herself in the mirror, leaving the maze of pink and white tiles behind her.

Meena and Javi were waiting for her under their big tree on the front lawn.

"Where the hell have you been?" Javi asked as she threw her backpack against the trunk, making a small pile with theirs. "Doesn't matter, listen to this. You know that creep Peterson? The shop teacher?"

"Yeah, I mean, I never took his class but I know who he is. Why?" Eli said, trying to keep her voice light, even, tell-me-more, trying not to look at Meena.

"Apparently some vigilante is going for revenge. Adrestia be with us."

"What do you mean?"

"Adrestia is the goddess of just retribution; she's the daughter of Ares and—"

"What is happening here in this century?" Eli asked.

"Oh, well, he's a total creepster, and everyone knows it. But they've all been too scared to say anything. But today, apparently there were like twelve-foot posters in his classroom calling him a child molester, and the whole team got texts and emails telling them to come forward with the truth about what a jerk he is."

"This is bullshit, Javi. No way." But this version of events was very entertaining.

"I'm telling you, that's what happened."

"Who did you hear it from?"

"Cherise, who got it from Becca, who got it from Tiffany, who was totally there when it all went down."

"When what all went down?"

"Charmaine called the cops."

"That did not happen."

"Maybe not, but I bet they're going to."

A strange calm settled over Eli. They lay for an hour at least under the tree, talking, laughing, taking pictures of each other, and telling Meena she should be a model.

"Seriously, look at this selfie," said Javi.

"You should do it for us, Meena. You could buy a mansion when you're eighteen, and we'll come and live in it."

"You have to look out for your less looks-privileged friends."

"Ugly kids deserve mansions too!" Eli and Javi cackled.

The slam of a car door made them turn their heads just in time to see Charmaine and her parents walking into school very, very slowly. There were tears on Charmaine's face, and she was still in her soccer uniform.

"Oh my god," said Javi.

"Do you think . . . ?" Meena couldn't finish her question, and looked at Eli. Eli said nothing; her heart had flown right into her mouth. She could feel it beating behind her teeth.

"Charmaine Wilson is comic-book-villain evil," said Javi. "But this is breaking my heart."

"My thoughts exactly," said Meena.

When Eli got home, Anna was chopping zucchini for lasagna.

"Do you have any idea what you're doing?" asked Eli.

"Well, no, but there's this thing called the internet . . ."

"Hardy-har-har."

"And also it's vegetables and noodles and cheese and tomato sauce. I mean, what could go wrong?"

"Please don't make me answer that."

"None for you then."

"Shut up and let me chop something."

The girls cooked in happy silence. When Anna's phone started ringing and buzzing, and every form of social media started popping up with alert after alert, Eli's stomach turned into a fist and then just one enormous knot.

Anna was sitting on the couch now, her tomato sauce abandoned. She wasn't speaking. She was just scrolling. And scrolling. And scrolling.

"Eli."

Eli kept chopping garlic. She stirred Anna's sauce. She did anything but answer.

"Eli, get in here ... Eli, I swear if you don't get your ass in here right now."

Eli sat down on the other side of the couch. She tried to stay very still and very calm, the way the dog trainers on Animal Planet did.

"Eli, what the hell did you do?"

"What are you talking about?"

"I am talking about #keepyourhandsoffme, which is *trending* right now. I am talking about the forty-seven, no wait, fifty-one Instagram posts of girls talking about Peterson. I am talking about the Snapchat of Charmaine walking into school in her uniform with her lawyer mother. I am talking about the fact that I told you to tell no one, and look what you did."

"I didn't tell anyone."

"Don't lie to me, Eli, not about this."

"Anna, I swear, I didn't say anything to anyone."

"I'm just supposed to believe that. I'm just supposed to believe that it's a big old coincidence that after I tell you what I've never told anyone, it's on the freaking internet."

"You don't have to believe me, but it's the truth. I would never tell anyone what you told me. Do any of these posts say anything about you? Does Charmaine Wilson even know you? I have literally never spoken to her."

"I never should have trusted you. I didn't need to be saved, Eli. I needed a sister."

Anna grabbed her hoodie off the chair and let the front door slam behind her. Eli didn't want to be home alone. The house felt too empty. Or maybe too full. Everything in it reminded her of people who weren't there—first Sam, then Mom, now Anna. She texted Meena:

Want to come over? I made lasagna.

Hours seemed to pass while she stared at her screen, waiting for Meena to write back.

Can't. Family game night. Come here!

Family game night. Basically the opposite of Eli's house right now. Meena's parents wouldn't mind; Eli would get her own bowl of popcorn and, as the guest, she'd get to choose which Monopoly piece she wanted to be (the shoe). But she also wanted to be home in case Anna decided to forgive her and come back. Unlikely, but still. Eli turned on the TV, turned up the volume. It was some old rerun of some sitcom; she didn't bother to see which one. She just let the sound of a TV family's laughter fill the living room and distract her as she scrubbed the kitchen until it shone.

* * *

It was after midnight when the phone rang. Eli had managed to fall asleep at the kitchen table where she had set herself up to wait. It was Anna. Or rather, it was Anna's butt. Eli couldn't hear anything but loud music and loud voices.

"Anna!" she shouted into the noise. The line went dead. Anna had sat down, she guessed. Eli texted her:

You okay?

ferhgu sidfbab came Anna's reply. She was drunk. It wasn't that Eli didn't understand that being a snoop was wrong, that it had occasionally terrible consequences, some of which she was experiencing at this very moment. But it was also truly, undeniably useful. She opened an app and started to trace Anna, entering her ID and password from carefully practiced memory. The icon appeared just where Eli feared, and she threw on her jacket and her shoes as quickly as she could.

She gripped her keys through her fingers the way Anna had showed her one night when they were walking home after looking for Mom, back when they still looked for her. Quiet streets, full moon, like a horror movie. She wished they had a dog, a big one, that she could walk with right now. She wanted to put in her headphones to distract herself from the fact that nighttime still made her afraid. But she needed to listen for footsteps behind her. Instead, every squirrel stepping on the smallest stick filled her with fear. Just go get Anna, Eli said to herself, go get Anna, get Anna, getanna, getanna, getanna. The Spotted Dog was a twenty-minute walk across town. Eli counted up to one hundred and back down again over and over until she was just outside. Where was Anna?

Eli pushed the heavy, black door open. It was dark inside, and it smelled like stale beer and cigarettes even though smoking had been banned here since before Eli was born. Most of all what it smelled like was familiar. Eli pushed Mom out of her mind. She just needed to find Anna. Eli put both hands on the bar and shouted to the bartender, "Matt, have you seen my sister?"

Matt had dated Mom for a while, about a year ago. He gave Eli a quick nod and pointed to the bathroom, just as friendly as he'd ever been. Jerk.

The bathroom was so bright after the dark bar, white lights on white walls on a white (or used-to-be-white floor). Eli spotted Anna's black boots in the third stall.

Last fall, when Anna still played soccer and Eli had no friends, Matt had texted Anna at 1:00 A.M. Eli was spooned against her when the pillow vibrated.

"What is it?" Anna asked as Eli reached for Anna's phone.

[102   ]

"It's Matt. We have to go get Mom."

They walked across the sleepy, silent town, everyone where they should be but Mom. Anna had put up a fight when Eli had started getting dressed. "It's fine, Eli, I don't need you to come," Anna had muttered, but Eli just put on her baseball cap and waited for Anna at the door. As they walked, they each woke up a little more, Anna walking faster as she grew angrier, Eli picking at her fingernails. When they got there, Mom was passed out on the bar.

Matt said, "Thanks for coming, guys. I couldn't let her drive home like this."

What a hero, Eli thought.

"Yeah, it'd be hard for her to drive, seeing as she's unconscious," Anna said. "Maybe next time, just don't give her so much alcohol."

"She's a paying customer, honey."

"And aren't you her boyfriend? Shouldn't you maybe give a shit about her?"

Matt moved to the other end of the bar to take an order.

"Come on, Mom." Eli shook Mom's shoulder. She didn't stir. Anna reached over the bar, grabbed a glass and filled it with water. She poured it over Mom's head.

Mom spluttered, "What the hell?" She shook like a wet dog.

"What the hell is that you're drunk and we're going home." Anna put an arm around Mom and eased her off the barstool. Eli lifted Mom's other arm over her shoulder. They walked her out to the car and put her in the backseat.

"She's totally going to puke all over the car," said Anna, getting into the driver's seat.

"Um, not to be rude, but you can't drive."

"Someone has to." And that was the night that Anna learned to drive. Eli could still see Anna's French braid pressing against the headrest as they herked and jerked all the way home. Near dawn, they put on the matching pajamas that were getting too small for both of them and curled up for what would be the last time under the celebratory grin of Abby Wambach.

Now here Anna was, splayed out on the formerly white tiles of the world's grossest, brightest bathroom. Eli wet a paper towel in the sink and kicked open the stall door.

"Anna," Eli said. "I know you're pissed at me but damn."

"Shhhh," said Anna, holding one limp hand in front of where she thought Eli's face was.

"Let's get you home."

"Shhhh," Anna said, to herself this time.

Eli struggled to get Anna to her feet, all gangly limbs and sharp corners. Anna hit her head on the metal stall. "Easy," said Eli, like she was building a very large, very wobbly tower of blocks.

"I'm fine," said Anna, though it sounded more like "ompine."

"Sure you are. Let's go home." Eli put her arm around Anna's waist and led her past the bar. The TV overhead showed Peterson walking out of the school holding a newspaper over his face. At least that meant he wouldn't be here tonight.

"Good night, Reynolds Sisters," Matt said as they made their way to the door.

Eli flipped him off.

"Like mother, like daughter," she swore she heard him say.

Outside, Eli shifted Anna to her arm, holding up her tall skinniness as they made their way down the sidewalk. At the first corner, Eli felt Anna's entire body lurch and held her over the sewer grate.

"I'm good," Anna slurred as she came to standing.

"Yeah, you're great. Come on." Eli said, guiding her home. Anna puked at the next sewer grate. Another fifteen blocks to go. She puked on the bushes by the public library. Ten blocks.

"That's it," Anna said. "No more." They moved down the sidewalk in a strange, silent dance the rest of the way home.

"Almost there," Eli said as they started to slowly climb the stairs up to their apartment. Inside, Eli got Anna a big glass of water and two Advils and put her to bed. She propped Anna's head up and to the side, just in case the puking wasn't really done, and put a trash can by her bed. She turned off the light.

"PB," Anna said as Eli was closing the door.

"Yeah, Banana?"

"Lasagna."

"Yeah, I made lasagna."

"I'm still mad."

"I know."

"Not at you."

"Good night."

—12—

AT TEN ON Saturday morning, Jason knocked on the door. At first, Eli thought it was part of her dream. Her second thought was that it was a cop. But then she remembered that Mom was in rehab. The thoughts came in like water from a tap after that: Mom's in rehab, we have no money, Anna hates me kind of. And there's Jason the Leather Jacket at the front door.

"Hi," Eli said through the screen.

"Hey, you must be Eli."

"And you're the . . . you're Jason."

"I am. Your sister up?"

"She will be once she knows you're here. Please hold." Eli closed the door and went to give Anna the good news. Hopefully this would calm her. Then they could tackle the whole having-no-money problem. Anna's dark room smelled like a hangover, stale and too sweet. Anna's room needed a shower.

"Anna, I know you hate me, but Jason's here and you'd hate me more if I didn't get you up."

"Shhhh."

"Anna. The Jacket, the one and only Jacket, is standing in our doorway asking for you. Get up."

Anna's hand reached out from the depths of her gray sheets. She put her full weight in Eli's hands and dragged herself out of bed, blinking hard, opening and closing her mouth in disbelief. "He's *here?*"

"Yes, like, on the porch. Do you want me to let him in?"

"Just tell him I'll be right there." At the rate Anna had started moving, that might actually be true. Before Eli could get to the front door, Anna looked like herself (her new self, anyway): black tank top, hoodie. Eli heard the tap running. It was possible that Anna was applying eyeliner and brushing her teeth at the same time. This version of Anna was so far from the mess on the bathroom floor last night that Eli wondered for a second if she'd made it up. Eli was still shaking her head when she got to the Jacket.

"She'll be right there," she said. Jason nodded and gave a half grin. Eli shook her head. She imagined Anna falling literally head first over her heels and laughed to herself.

In a flash, Anna emerged from the bathroom, looking bright-eyed and smelling way better than she deserved to.

"I'll see you later," she said to Eli.

"Where are you going?"

"Where are we going, Jason?" she asked.

"World's our oyster. Wherever your heart desires."

"You heard him—wherever my heart desires, Eli. I'll text you." And just like that, they were gone.

Having the house to herself wouldn't be a bad thing, Eli figured. She turned on some music and told herself that she was going to clean. And she was. But this was a snooping expedition dressed up as chores, and she knew it. She vacuumed the rug in the living room. She opened the curtains. She opened the windows. She breathed in the warm spring air and thought about Meena. She wondered where Jason and Anna would go, and how it was possible to dream of a person and talk about a person and imagine kissing a person and let your sister and your friends tease you about a person because the very idea of them is too good to be true and then for them to just show up on your porch on a hungover Saturday spring morning because *that person* wanted to see *you*. How did that happen?

Hello, people.

Eli started the group chat. Meena texted back.

E-licious! I'm working with my chem group. See you later maybe? 👧 🧪 💥

Of course Meena was with her chem group. Chem group was a class at the community college for middle school and high school students with a special interest in the sciences. Meena had been a member since she was in sixth grade. Once they started high school next year, she could finally compete for a spot on their robotics team. She was a phenomenal dork with a phenomenal smile.

You guys suck. Mandatory brunch with the fam in Springfield. It's going to be a hundred years until I'm free again.

Javi's family had mandatory brunches every few months. He hated them, and they always took all day. Maybe Eli knew that today was one of those days. Maybe that's why she'd texted, hoping Meena would text back with an offer to hang out, that Javi wouldn't be able to attend. Maybe.

Hi to the fam, A. Thank Biff for lending me his cool threads the other night. M, I'm around later if you and the mad scientists don't blow us all to bits.

Eli slid her phone into her pocket and smiled. Later. For now, time to change the sheets and try to get

[110]

some air to circulate in Anna's room. She even made herself clean the toilet before she let herself get down to business. Business was Mom's room. With Anna gone for god-knows-how-long with the Jacket, and Meena busy until at least this afternoon, she had time to dig. Starting with the mail that had accumulated on the bed, she pocketed the new unemployment check, five hundred and fifty dollars total. Not enough for rent, not enough for much, but enough to keep them eating and driving for a few weeks. She found their report cards and forged Mom's signature without even looking at the grades. This was not real snooping. Real snooping was opening every drawer of the nightstand and going through each one slowly. Eli approached each drawer methodically, like Meena going through the steps of an experiment. The box of condoms didn't embarrass her; when she was snooping, it didn't feel like she was even a person. She was gathering data. She was processing information. There's no room for embarrassment in an investigation.

She had never given herself permission to do a full-on snoop attack on Mom's room. Usually, she'd just sneak in to grab her paycheck twenty and stash it. She'd always thought that Mom would somehow know if she went through the drawers that always beckoned her with their undone locks, half-open and dark. Or, more likely, that Anna would catch her and tell her about kiddie jail and her doomed future if she kept up this snooping. But Anna was out. And Mom was in rehab. And there was information to gather.

After the condoms, the wrung-out bottles of skin cream, and a few empty airplane bottles of booze that didn't come from any airplane, in one of the old magazines Eli found a picture of Sam. He was blond and broad, with a wide smile just like her own. In the next drawer, there was an old picture that she had never seen before. A little girl, who must have been Mom, standing with the actual Aunt Lisa and a skinny, sharp-faced woman who must have been their mom. These all went into the keep pile, with the report cards and the unemployment check. By the end of the afternoon, that pile grew to include six letters from LR (seven when she added the one she'd pocketed the other day); seven postcards from Sam addressed to Eli and Anna, each with different states on the front and no return address; a picture of a tall, skinny man with dark hair and blue eyes; and an old address book. No one used address books anymore, but it was data. And you never knew when you might really need some data.

When Meena texted for her to come over, Eli stuffed all her data into her red backpack and threw it under her bed. She hopped on her bike to her favorite TV family's house. The Patels could have their own sitcom, and Eli would have happily binge-watched it. As she pulled in the driveway, Meena's dad was washing the car and spraying the hose at her little brother and sister in between cleaning the wiper blades. An alternate universe just a bike ride away.

Meena opened the door. "Please ignore the freaks and just come inside."

Her dad sprayed the hose in the direction of the house.

"Dad, stop!" she yelled, smiling, as she brought Eli inside. Meena's room was at the top of the stairs, clean with big windows looking out to the tall trees in the backyard. It reminded Eli of a tree house. Meena threw herself onto the enormous green beanbag in the corner of her room.

"Come on," she said to Eli, patting the spot next to her. "Look at me blowing stuff up in the lab this morning."

Eli laughed and sat down. She couldn't help but notice that their knees touched every time Eli leaned over to see the video. Her jeans against Meena's leggings, and then away, and then against, and then away, and then against. They stayed like that for hours, watching videos and talking, the room growing dark and neither one getting up to turn on the light.

"What do you want to be, E-licious?"

"Well, not a mad scientist; I'll leave that to you. I don't know." Eli leaned her head back. "But I want to do it far away from here."

"Hell yes," said Meena. "We'll go to the West Coast for college, stay out there. Work on a ranch in the summers."

"Do I look like I can work on a ranch?" Eli laughed, but secretly thought, we, we, we.

"I think you'd look cute with a tan and a cow."

"I bet you say that to all the girls." Eli laughed, elbowing Meena.

"No," Meena said, suddenly serious. "Just to you."

Eli had been staring at the small crack in the ceiling right above them for a few minutes now, but Meena's tone brought her right down. She looked over to her, their faces inches, or were they centimeters, apart, the corners of her mouth contemplating a smile. Eli swallowed hard, her heart beating fast. She fought the urge to close her eyes and shake her head, just to make sure this would all still be happening when she opened them again. Instead, she looked at Meena, at the stars through the trees over her shoulder, at her big eyes in this dark room. She kissed her. It was short maybe, or maybe long. She had nothing to compare it to except for the queen at *Rocky Horror*, and this wasn't that.

Eli didn't hear the door open. She just felt Meena's hands on her shoulders suddenly pushing her away.

"Eli, stop," Meena said, looking away from her, frowning. Disgusted.

"What?" Eli asked, confused. That's when she noticed the open door. It was Meena's father, who didn't call her "sport" now, bellowing, "What's going on in here?" and saying, "You need to go, Eliza."

—13—

BY MONDAY, ELI was starting to think that she'd made up the kiss. In some ways, that was better—it meant that its ending was made up too. Meena had texted her that night, a sad face. What did that mean? Sad that I kissed you? Sad that your dad hates me now? Sad that you looked at me like I was a freak the second he opened the door? Eli didn't respond. Anna still wasn't home. She had sent a text, at least:

Gonna stay at Jason's tonight. u good?

Eli sent back a thumbs-up and an eggplant emoji. No reason to ruin Anna's good time. But then she didn't text Sunday and now it was Monday and the house was too empty. Everything seemed as broken and sad as she was. The wall clock that had said 3:43 since October made her want to cry. She dragged herself to the bus, dragged herself to school. She didn't stop and look for Javi and Meena. She saw Kevin's hat through the door and walked in anyway. Whatever he was going to do or say to her this morning wouldn't matter, wouldn't make it worse.

"Hey boy, where's your girlfriend?" Kevin shouted at her as soon as she was through the double door.

"Fuck off, Kevin," she growled.

"What's that, boy?" He grabbed her elbow and started pushing her towards the bathroom. For a second, for ten seconds, she let him. Screw it.

"I said fuck off, you homophobic moron. Get a hobby. Why do you care where I pee? What are you, eight? I mean, I know your IQ is. I guess that explains it."

"Bad mood, huh?" he said as he kicked open the door. "I guess your girlfriend Meena's getting tired of dykes like you."

Eli didn't know she could throw a punch. Kevin fell back against the door, holding his jaw. Pain coursed up and down Eli's hand as Principal Calderón appeared by her side.

It was impossible to explain it, even though they kept asking. Principal Calderón and Mr. Sposato sat across from her, all kind eyes and concern, and asked her to tell them what happened.

"You're a good kid, Eli," Principal Calderón kept saying. "This isn't like you, Eli."

"You don't know me," she said, looking down. Sometimes, she thought, when the walls of your life are crashing around you, the only thing to do is pull them down on top of you.

"You've sat at my dinner table and slept on my couch, Eli. You're no stranger, but I don't recognize you right now."

"You're not that easy to know." That was Mr. Sposato, trying a different tactic. Trying, like he always did. "But I think Javi and Meena do; I think your Aunt Lisa does. And I think all of them would be surprised by what happened this morning."

Meena's name made pinpricks behind her eyes. Please stop, she thought.

"We can help you, Eli."

"That's bullshit." And another wall crashed down, bricks smashing against her ribs.

"Oh, Eli. I'm sorry to do this." Principal Calderón sounded genuinely sorry. "This school has a no-tolerance policy when it comes to violence. Your clean record may let you off with a lighter consequence, but your attitude isn't helping. I'll call your mother, and you'll be home for the rest of the week. Are we clear?"

Eli wasn't clear on anything. Except for the fact that no one would be home to answer Principal Calderón's call. She saw the phone ringing in her empty house, Anna nowhere to be found, no Mom to show up for the meeting Principal Calderón would surely want to have, just a phone ringing and ringing into the dark. She got up, slammed the office door, hoping the glass would break, and ran out of the building, down the street, past the bus stop, until she couldn't breathe.

The house was empty and dark. As always. She crawled into bed with her clothes and shoes on.

When she woke up it was dark outside and inside. There was a text from Javi on the group chat:

E, did you really kick his ass? Yaaas, regina. My mom's not even mad. She knows he had it coming.

Then Meena:

Are you okay?

Eli fought the urge to throw her phone. No, I'm not okay. There was a message on their landline from the school, asking for Mom to call.

What there wasn't, was Anna. She texted:

are you ever coming home?

She called. Straight to voicemail. Her phone was off. Of course. She typed texts and deleted them:

(Hope you're having fun, but we have literally no food. Other people exist besides Jason, you know. Banana, please come home.)

She turned her phone off and fell back asleep.

In the morning, there was a box of donuts on the table, some milk in the fridge, and a note from Anna saying she'd be home late, that Eli should eat without her. Eli crumpled the note and threw it in the trash. She didn't want to eat the donut, as if by refusing her offer, she could compel Anna to come to her senses and come home. But she was hungry, and it was a donut. She ate it. It tasted like nothing. It was too weird to sit in the house all day, thinking of what Meena and Javi were doing, her day cut up into forty-five-minute sections that meant nothing without the bells, the classes, the noise, and the two sides to her triangle that made it all bearable. She took another donut and walked out the door.

The bus to Green Hills wasn't one bus; it was three, and a mile walk from the last stop. The bus rides went by in a blur, Eli tucked into her hoodie, just watching streaks of highway wash by. Her phone buzzed in her backpack. Meena. Javi. Meena and Javi. She turned it off. Her stomach grumbled. The donuts were a nice touch but if Anna didn't show up with some actual groceries soon, it was going to be graham crackers and one last can of soup for the foreseeable future. She didn't mind the empty feeling in her stomach; it didn't feel that different from the rest of her today anyway.

Eli woke up with a jolt at the last stop—that startled moment when you don't remember where you are, or that you were sleeping. The walk to Green Hills went by on autopilot, like she was watching some other thirteen-year-old make her way down that odd stretch of highway between exits 17B and 17C to streets with no sidewalks. When she turned up the street to Green Hills, Eli thought she'd feel relief, a weight lifted, some hope from this brick beacon on a not-so-much hill. But she just felt more nothing.

The woman at the desk, wearing scrubs like this was an actual hospital, instead of just a place for people who are a different kind of sick to get a different kind of better, asked if she could help her.

"I'm looking for Carrie Reynolds." The woman typed for a while into a computer.

"Group B is out for the day, sweetheart. They're at a meeting until nine tonight. Come back this weekend for visiting hours."

Eli wasn't surprised (she wasn't anything) to find her legs turning the other way, back down to the streets and to the weird stretch of highway between exits 17C and 17B. Of course Mom wasn't there. Eli couldn't remember why she'd come here in the first place. It wasn't like Mom was going to be able to help. She couldn't even help herself. She was sitting in a church basement somewhere getting the help that she needed. Eli didn't want to sit in the cafeteria and look at Mom's sad eyes over lukewarm hot chocolate, smelling that faint hospital smell and looking at the thick, dark roots of Mom's hair that had grown out since her last dye job.

Eli heard honking behind her as she crossed the street to the highway ramp. Great, she thought, now I'm going to get kidnapped by some hick. A beat-up blue pickup crept up beside her. But it wasn't a hick. Or at least not an unfamiliar one. It was Cliff, Mom's counselor from Green Hills.

"Hey, bookworm," he said as he rolled down the passenger-side window. Literally rolled it down, with a crank. How old was this piece of junk?

"Hey, psycho, you nearly ran me off the road."

"Get in."

What the hell, she figured, and she opened the creaky door. Inside, the cab of the truck smelled warm, like burnt wood or old leather.

"You seem like you could use a milkshake."

They rode in silence most of the way. Eli wasn't going to spill her guts to basically a stranger, but her stomach wasn't going to let her say no to free food either. Cliff pulled into Sal's Diner, right off the highway. They sat at the counter, Cliff looking at the menu as if he hadn't been here a million times, and Eli picking at the peeling formica.

"Their waffle fries are aces," Cliff said.

"I'm not that hungry."

Cliff laughed. "Right, and you're having a great day too. Don't try to bullshit a bullshitter, honey."

Eli smiled out of the corner of her mouth farthest from Cliff.

Cliff called to the waitress. "Could I get some coffee and a tuna melt, Alice? And whatever my surly friend here would like." Alice looked like a diner waitress from the movies—blond hair pulled back into a ponytail, little weird paper hat on her head, uniform, apron, white sneakers. Up close, Eli could see that she had a small triangle tattoo on her wrist and a gold tooth.

"Strawberry milkshake, cheeseburger, and waffle fries, please." She didn't look at Cliff, didn't want to see his grin.

"Too bad you're not—"

"Shut up," Eli said, almost laughing for the first time in days.

"So, what brings you to Green Hills? Looking for some Grade A rehabilitation?"

"I don't know."

"Well, neither do I, but if you're willing to take a million buses and walk along the highway to get here, it's probably not because you're having the time of your life. Just a guess."

"Yeah, not really. It's just been a bad couple of days."

"I've had some of those."

"Yeah, but . . ."

"But I made those, and this is just happening to you?"

"Kinda, yeah. Mom always says that she has bad days, but then it's like she goes out and pours alcohol all over the bad day, which obviously makes everything worse, and then she stands around being like, who made this terrible mess. She can't even see that she did it. I didn't do this."

"Whatever it is, I'm sure that you didn't do it. But even if you don't have a choice about what's happening, you have a choice about how you respond to it. You've got more power than you think, Eli. That's for damn sure."

They ate in the silence of the truly hungry and the truly happy. Eli fell asleep on the drive home, her doggie bag leaking its warm smell and just a little grease onto the floor by her feet. (If Anna happened to be home, Eli guessed she deserved dinner. If not, Eli would happily have a milkshake and French fries for breakfast.) Eli opened her eyes every few traffic lights to indicate left or right and Cliff hummed along with the classical music playing on the radio.

Eli didn't bother turning on the lights when she got home. The car still wasn't in the parking lot. She put the food in the fridge and saw a red light glowing from the landline. New messages. She'd check later.

—14—

AROUND 4:00 A.M. on Saturday, after a lonely week of stale leftover fries and seeing how long she could make one can of soup last, Eli heard the door creak open. She wanted to start the fight right then and there. She wanted to tell her sister that she could go right to hell for making her worry, for making her hungry, for leaving her alone for days on end. Instead, she was just mad at herself for being relieved to have Anna home. At 7:45, Eli finally listened to the answering machine and decided it was time for Anna to wake up. She poured an entire glass of water on her sister's sleeping head. "What the hell, Anna?"

"What the hell yourself, Eli? What the hell was that for?"

"It's for not coming home. It's for messages on the machine from school asking where you are. It's for the fact that you missed an entire week of school and now a social worker is coming to the house to check on us. Good job, Aunt Lisa. Do you not care about us at all? Is it just the Jacket that matters to you now? You smell terrible. Dye your hair and get dressed. You have to *seem* like a responsible adult by the afternoon. There's Advil in the bathroom, Mom."

The "Mom" was supposed to sting, but Anna didn't even seem to hear her. She just walked, slowly, into the bathroom. She turned on the light and squinted at her own reflection.

"You need to be in the shower already," Eli shouted towards the bathroom. Nothing came back. Even a "shut up" would be better than this. At least then she'd know that Anna was listening, but lately it seemed like Anna was on her own planet, a far better one, leaving Eli alone to deal with everything happening on Earth. She brought the coffee into the bathroom, where Anna was sitting on the toilet, staring lovingly at her phone.

"A little privacy?" Anna snapped, not looking up.

"Drink this. It's strong. Get in the shower. We don't have time for privacy. Or for anything else. If you care about me at all, get in the shower. Dye your hair. Act like you care about us." Eli turned on the shower and walked out, slamming the door behind her. Soooo immature, she could hear her sister thinking. But sometimes the door needed to be slammed. Sometimes it felt like the perfect punctuation mark. Maturity could wait for when there wasn't a social worker on the way to their house and when her sister came back from whatever planet she lived on now.

When they were little, Eli used to have a bag packed under her bed, just in case the kids from *Troop Invincible* came to recruit her. *Troop Invincible* was on every Saturday morning, and sometimes really late at night for reruns. It was about a runaway gang of kids who discovered their superhero powers. They lived together with Mulligan. Old and in a wheelchair, Mulligan had hidden his powers for most of his life, as his parents had kicked him out the first time he passed the salt and pepper using only his eyes. Mulligan ran a safe house for superpowered teens who didn't know where to turn.

Eli couldn't count the number of times she'd prayed to go there. Not that she had superpowers (unless you counted sneaking stuff and being not quite a girl, which she sometimes did), but Mulligan House was full of people and good food (an underrated superpower of Howdini, who could scale walls and also make perfect pancakes). The house was invisible to the naked eye and that had sounded perfect to six-year-old Eli. Her red backpack had a change of underwear, jeans, a sweatshirt, her favorite seven books, a hat and the dental hygiene kit they gave out at school so she'd be ready to go at a moment's notice, in case anyone ever offered her a bed at Mulligan House.

That same red backpack didn't hold quite as much now, but she grabbed it anyway. A shirt, underwear, a pair of shorts, her toothbrush. The letters from Mom's bed and the cash from the top of the fridge. She went into Anna's room, holding her nose, and looked for Anna's black backpack amid all the black clothes spread like carpet on her floor. She kicked the clothes out of the way until she found something not so easily kicked. She emptied out the backpack on the bed; a textbook and notebooks, pens, a lighter, and a shiny silver flask tumbled onto the soft gray sheets. She didn't have time to think about it now, to hear Cliff's voice in her head telling her to be careful, that this was hereditary. She didn't have time to feel jealous of the cool smooth that the flask naturally gave its holder; she didn't have time to wonder where it had come from or how many times it had been full and then empty. She picked up a few handfuls of clothes from the floor and stuffed them into the backpack.

There was a knock on the door. Not a cop knock; softer, but not Jason's knock—just as cool and casual as he was. Meena? The name stopped her heart.

"Eliza? Anna?" The voice—most definitely not Meena's (that name again, that skipped heartbeat)—came through the door. *Eliza.*

Eli walked into the bathroom. "Anna, how close to done are you?" She was whispering as loudly as she could to be heard over the shower.

"You've got to be kidding me. You send me in here and now you're rushing me out? This shit takes like two hours. Could I get a little space? Or is it time for another lecture? I'm sorry that my hair doesn't dye fast enough for y—"

"Stop talking."

"You're the only one who can talk? This is bull—"

"Seriously, Anna. Stop. Stop talking. Stop dyeing your hair. The social worker is here."

Anna's face appeared to side of the plastic curtain. "Like, *here* here?"

"Like, standing outside, knocking on the door, asking for Anna and Eliza."

"Fuck."

"Yeah. Get out of the shower."

"What are we doing?"

"Leaving."

Eli waited for Anna in Mom's room, by the back window that led to the fire escape that went to the ground. They would have to be fast. And lucky. She silently tossed Anna her black backpack as she opened the window. She held her finger to her lips. She gave Anna the car keys and nodded.

Getting to the ground was easy enough. Trying to do it without being seen or heard by neighbors wasn't as easy. Eli jumped first. She landed loud. Klutz, she thought angrily. She put up her hand, telling Anna to wait. The social worker didn't come running around the corner in what Eli knew would be sensible shoes and a long, corduroy skirt. She listened for rustling. She nodded to Anna, who seemed to float effortlessly from the bottom rung to the ground because of course she did. Older sisters.

They walked up to the corner of the building, poking their heads around like little kids playing hide-and-seek. They could see her sensible shoes on the stairs above them. The key was to get to the car—across the parking lot—before the social worker decided to give up and come another day.

"We just have to run for it," said Anna. And they did, Anna in the lead, her soccer days (and legs) not so far behind her after all. Eli lumbered after her, moving faster than she ever had. But not fast enough. Sensible

Shoes Social Worker turned around as Anna opened the driver's side door and Eli hit the ground, trying to hide between cars.

"Girls!" Sensible Shoes Social Worker called from the top of the stairs. "Anna! Eliza! I need to speak with you both!" She came down the stairs as Anna started the car. For a moment, Eli thought Anna would take off without her. The car screeched to a stop right in front of her.

"NOW!" Anna yelled.

Eli got up and got in, as SSSW ran—fast for a lady in a corduroy skirt—towards them, now only a few cars away. One-eighth in the tank, one hundred bucks in their backpacks, some toothpaste. *Go, go, go,* the wheels seemed to hum as they took corners at full force and blew through yellow-to-red lights. *Go, go, go.*

—15—

AT A GAS station outside of Centerville, they finally gave in to the flashing-yellow empty sign. As Anna pulled up and slowed down, everything came into focus.

"Wow," said Eli.

"Holy shit."

Anna got out of the car, patted her pockets for money, found some, and paid for gas. Eli stared at the cars going by. Anna got back in and started the car, but didn't move.

"I don't . . . Where are we going?"

"I have some ideas," said Eli. "But first we need money, we're running out. Do you think the Jacket can help us out?"

"How much do we need?"

"Depends on how long we'll be gone, which depends on where we go next."

Anna texted Jason.

Things are seriously screwed up at home. I know this sounds weird, but could you lend me some money?

A text bubble appeared immediately.

Not weird. Meet me at my uncle's store in 20.

Jason's uncle's store was in the wrong direction. Wrong because it was in Middletown, wrong because it meant driving back—not near the apartment exactly, but close enough that neither girl spoke on the drive there. Anna parked around back, and without being told to, Eli slid down to the floor while she waited, one ear out for SSSW and for the romantic good-bye she knew her sister would be having with Jason.

Jason's uncle ran a liquor store, and Jason worked there on the weekends. He came out with a paper bag and a deep kiss for Anna. She put her hands inside his back pockets.

"There's about two hundred bucks in here; that's all I could get."

"Please tell me you didn't steal this," she said.

"I didn't. He owed me for a few weekends. I collected."

"I'm going to pay you back."

"I know you will. But you should know that sometimes it's nice to let people help you. Especially the people who love you."

"I have to go." Eli heard Anna's voice struggle to sound firm.

"What's going on?"

Eli sat back up as Anna kissed him long and hard and got in the car without another word. Eli didn't look at her. This was the reason that Anna had left her alone for six days with donuts and an occasional text message. She was glad for the money but she didn't want to see her sister blink back tears for the person who had torn what was left of their family apart.

Sunset came by surprise. The girls watched the sun go down from Scoby Diner a few towns away. Not enough towns away, not really. Eli had thought about calling Javi; he would have let them sleep at his house—he probably would have emptied King Douchebag's wallet to help them out. But she couldn't bear the idea of dragging him into this—and it would be hard for Principal Calderón to explain to the school board why she was harboring two fugitives from Social Services. Eli wouldn't let herself think about calling Meena. She wouldn't be able to do anything for them anyway, and even if she could, her father would never let her.

Diners were magical; Eli and Anna both knew it was true. The warm smell of something greasy cooking all day, the inexhaustible menu. At a diner, anything seemed possible—pancakes at midnight, a Nicoise salad, the perfect onion ring. They stared at the enormous menus from opposite sides of their booth.

"What can I get for you, girls?"

"French toast and a root beer float, please."

"Eli, you need to eat protein or you're not going to make it through the night. Bring her some chicken fingers too, please. And a chicken Caesar wrap and fries for me, please."

The waitress made her way to the next booth. Eli hissed, "I don't need you trying to tell me what to eat, but thanks."

"Listen, it's going to be a long night. You're going to start moaning at eleven that you're hungry, and we can't be out by ourselves late at night without drawing a lot of attention."

"So now you care. I've been taking care of myself perfectly well for the last week without your help."

"I'm sorry."

"Save it."

"You want to be mad at me, that's fine. But we have to get through this together. Look around Eli, you see anyone else here to make it through with? You're stuck with me. Like it or don't."

"I don't."

"No shit."

The food came, hot and old at the same time. When Anna got up to go to the bathroom, Eli secretly and resentfully ate a chicken finger. From Scoby's they drove without talking and without a plan—just anywhere that wasn't Middletown. Anywhere they could spend the night undetected, undisturbed, unseparated. Anna went north on 16, and then west on 47. The towns went from copies of Middletown to others that seemed only to have houses like Meena's and Javi's, with manicured lawns and trashless playgrounds. They had downtowns with movie-set brick buildings that matched the exact hue of the eerily symmetrical brick sidewalks, restaurants boasting "farm to table" on sidewalk blackboards, and multiple "artisan crafts" stores.

"Where the hell are we?"

"The fancy part."

"Apparently."

"Are they going to tow our car just for looking out of place?"

"Holy shit, Eli, look at that." Down the hill from them, Fairview High School didn't look anything like

MHS, or any other high school they'd seen. It looked like a college. Or like a spaceship. Its white dome gleamed in the night. You could still hear the cheers from their three (three!) sports fields. "I was going to say we could park here and sleep, but I bet they have their own security detail just to keep the riffraff out."

They drove around looking for the best place to park. A mall? What about a bar? A car wouldn't stand out but there'd be too much foot traffic. No need to attract any concerned citizens. As they came to the outskirts of Fairview, Anna spotted it.

"There," she said. Eli nodded. "Be as mad as you want; I'm brilliant." Eli didn't disagree. They pulled up next to the car dealership, shut down for the night with cars spilling into the street. Anna found a spot between two parked cars.

"Gotta say I'm brilliant but this is still creepy AF."

"Yup," said Eli, pulling her hood up.

"It's one night," said Anna.

"What happens tomorrow night?"

"I don't know. But not this."

They each put their seats back and settled into their phones, not looking up or speaking. Eli put on old Radiohead and Anna said nothing, so Eli knew she really *did* feel guilty. Eli played Candy Crush until she saw candy pieces on the insides of her eyelids when she blinked, while Anna scrolled and scrolled and scrolled.

Eli's alarm was set for six but she woke up at five. During the night, she and Anna had linked arms. She took her arm back and opened her backpack. She took out the letters, the pictures, the postcards, and the address book.

"What's all that?" Anna asked, when the sun woke her later. She rubbed her eyes, smudging her makeup.

"Let's get you caffeinated. It's time to hatch a plan."

Eli and Anna took turns in the Dunkin' Donuts bathroom. Eli brushed her teeth, splashed water on her face and under her arms and went to wait for Anna who took forever. When she reappeared, Eli noticed what the extra minutes had gone to.

"Really, Anna? A cat eye when you're on the run?"

"Really. Now, show me what my sneak of a sister has in store for me."

"Well, as far as I can tell, we have three options. There's actual Aunt Lisa," Eli said, pointing to a stack of letters. "She's been writing to Mom once every few months since they stopped talking."

"What do the letters say?"

"What do you take me for, a monster? I needed her address, not her innermost thoughts."

"What do they say?"

"Mostly that she misses Mom, misses us, and doesn't understand why Mom won't talk to her. Turns out she does live in Oxbridge, Vermont, Mom didn't make it up."

"Vermont is seven hours from here."

"It's six hours and forty-six minutes according to Google."

"That's a hell of a lot of gas."

"My thoughts exactly. But you might not like my next thought."

"What?" Anna's voice croaked with dread.

"I understand you might not want to do this, so I want to tell you right now, I will knock over this Dunkin' Donuts for gas money if I need to, you don't have to say—"

"Get to the point."

"This is a picture of your dad. His name is John." Holding her breath, Eli passed the picture across the table. Anna closed her eyes. She took a deep breath of her own, lowering her head without opening her eyes. When she finally opened them, she stared at the picture for a long, long time.

"Black hair," she said quietly, what seemed like hours later.

"Just like you said."

Anna looked at Eli quickly, the hint of a tear in her right eye; she smiled slightly and nodded. "I can't believe you remember that. Where is he?"

"He's in her address book, and who in the hell uses an address book, and when was the last time she was together enough to use one so who knows, but I think he lives in Fairview."

"We're in Fairview."

"Yeah."

"How far is he from this Dunkin' Donuts?"

"Eleven minutes."

"So you're telling me that our options are to drive for a million hours with gas we don't have or to drive five miles and meet my long-lost, deadbeat dad, who obviously has no interest in me since he's been maybe two hours away from us my entire life?"

"Like I said, I don't mind committing some larceny."

"What's the third option?"

"Well, that's less of an option."

"What is it?"

"These are postcards from Sam. They're from all over the country. The last one is from Wisconsin, but he sent it three years ago."

"Jesus, Eli, let's review the definition of the word *option* because you're using it wrong. Okay. Let's go find dear old Dad. This should be a helluva good time."

The eleven-minute drive felt like days. Time had lost its meaning: no school, no meals, no showers to set its march to. This part of Fairview was row after row of ranch houses, cars in the driveway, or in the garage, the occasional runner or kid on a bike. 68 Clarkson Road was a brown ranch with white trim and a well-watered lawn. There was no car in the driveway, but there was a kid's bike.

"Oh, perfect. He has no interest in being my dad, but he's totally down to be somebody else's," Anna practically spat.

"Nobody's home. Want to go spy?"

"No, but I know you do."

Eli hopped out of the car, happy to use the full range of motion of her legs again. "This way," she said as she ducked around the side of the house. This part of the yard had a small garden with sunflowers, their faces stretching to the sunny backyard. "You can't take one," she said to Anna, who was eyeing them angrily.

"I can take whatever I want," she snarled, but she left them alone.

Through the window, they could see the inside of the garage. Old suitcases, gardening equipment, roller skates, a deflated beach ball and umbrella. Everything slightly messy but unmistakably happy. Eli could feel Anna growing angrier.

"Come on," she said, leading Anna around to the back. The backyard had a swing set and another garden. The sun shone on the grass, and their noses filled with the smell of clean air and morning. Eli stopped short. A man was sitting on the back patio, coffee in his hand. One look at him—that tall, skinny body and shock of black hair—and Eli knew just who he was. Anna did too. Eli could feel her start to turn around.

"Um, hello?" the man called out. "Can I help you?"

"Oh, I think we got lost, sorry. We were looking for my grandmother's house, must have the wrong one, our mistake," said Eli, as she backed up.

"No, Eli," Anna whispered. "Screw this. Screw him. He can know who I am." She took a breath, and stepped in front of Eli. "My name is Anna Reynolds, Carrie Reynolds's daughter. Your daughter."

He said nothing at first. Just hung his mouth open.

"Oh my god," Anna said. "You don't even know about me, do you?"

"I don't. I didn't." He took a deep breath, recovering himself. "But I'm glad to now. Come. Sit. Please."

Anna and Eli took the short-yet-long walk over to the picnic table on the patio and sat across from him.

"I'm John Regis," he said.

"We know," they said.

"This is Eli," said Anna. "My sister. Don't worry, she's not yours."

"It's nice to meet you, Eli. Anna, I don't know what to say. You look just like . . ."

"Like if you and my mom had a baby?"

He laughed. "Kind of, yeah."

"I know. So you didn't know about me?"

"No, I would have . . . You would know me if I had known about you."

The three sat in silence.

"Where's your wife?" asked Anna.

"She took our son to the beach early this morning. She's, um, she's about to have a baby."

"You're having another baby."

"We are."

"Boy or girl?"

"A girl. Then there's, Zack. He's six."

"Good for you."

"Anna, I had no idea. I'm so sorry. I would love to know you. How's your mom? Do you guys want something to drink? Something to eat? Let's go inside."

They walked the few steps into the house, and Eli whispered, "He's nervous. Be nicer."

The kitchen was big, with an island and a table with four chairs, a stainless-steel fridge covered in family pictures and the kid's art. The walls were painted yellow by the sun streaming through the windows. The girls sat at the island as John flitted around the kitchen, handing them glasses of iced tea and putting some muffins in the middle. Eli wanted to reach for one; she could feel her stomach grumbling.

"My wife, she likes to bake," he said awkwardly as he took milk out of the fridge. Eli noticed Anna's nails digging into her jeans like a cat with its claws out and decided against the muffin.

"So, what happened? Why didn't you stay with her?" Anna was just short of growling now.

"She left me."

"What are you talking about?"

"I was a senior and she was a junior. It was the end of my senior year, and I was headed away for college. Your mom and I, you know, we didn't come from much. My parents didn't go to college; most of the people I was graduating with weren't going to college. But I had gotten this big scholarship to the University of Massachusetts and I was going, but I had every intention of staying with Carrie. We had been together since the beginning of the year, and I figured one year and then she could join me at college. She is so smart, your mom—she didn't even realize how smart she was but you could tell; she had your number the minute she laid eyes on you." He got quiet then, staring into his coffee cup, talking about Mom like she was young, like she was extraordinary, like she was precious.

"Anyway, her mom had never been very supportive—I don't know if she talks about that. I don't want to speak ill of your grandmother."

"She died before Eli was born. I don't remember her. Mom doesn't talk about her much."

"I'm sorry to hear that. Wait, no I'm not. Honestly, she was a difficult woman with a serious drinking problem who put your mom down every chance she got. I always assumed that she was the real reason that Carrie broke up with me. That her mom had gotten into her head, convinced her that she could never hack it at college, and that she'd be better off at home. Now, though, I see that—"

"That I'm why she broke up with you."

"Carrie wouldn't have wanted me to sacrifice my scholarship to raise you—and please believe me that if she had told me that day that she was pregnant, I would have unloaded my car, unpacked my bags, and helped the best I could have. We were so young. You must be—"

"I'm seventeen."

"You're older than she was when I left."

"I know. I'm good at math."

"You get that from her. The sharp tongue too." Anna smiled just a little. Eli kicked her lightly under the table. "So, I went to college. I was heartbroken that she didn't want to be with me. I tried to find her when I'd come home for school breaks but she wouldn't answer the phone, and I finally figured that she really must not want to see me, and so I let her be."

"Did you graduate? Was it worth it?"

"Nothing is worth not knowing you, or having your mother struggle like that alone. How is she? Does she know you're here?"

"She doesn't know we're here. She's . . . having a hard time."

"Hard times run in the family, I guess." His phone started to ring. "Sorry, excuse me."

"Are you okay?" Eli whispered.

"I don't know. This is weird. I want him to be a jerk. Why is he not a jerk?"

"So weird."

John came back in the room, face flushed and smiling, sweat beading at his forehead.

"Guys, I'm sorry to do this, but my wife is having the baby. I really want to continue this conversation, and to be a part of your life if you'll have me, but right now I have to go to the hospital. The hospital. Oh my god. She has my car."

"We have a car. We can drive you," Anna said, meeting his eyes for the first time. He put his hand on top of hers.

"Thank you."

At the hospital, John thanked the girls again before getting out of the car. "I want to see you again—this is my number. Call anytime. And please tell Carrie I said hello, and that I hope the hard time gets easier. In the meantime, I know it's not much, but it's all I had at home." He handed Anna a small wad of cash.

"I wasn't coming here for money," she said, which wasn't technically true, but had become true.

"I know you weren't. But family looks out for each other. It's the least I can do. Take good care of yourselves. And of your mom." And he was gone, swallowed up by the rotating doors of the emergency room, running to find his wife. A siren screamed as an ambulance pulled up behind the car, and Anna drove off.

—16—

SPRING IN NEW ENGLAND was green, even
on the highway. Stretches of highway and winding
roads and more highway ahead. The green trees gave
way to more green trees. Eli started categorizing them—
dark, mint, lime, olive, emerald. Javi would know more.
Summer was on its way; you could tell by the sweet air
and the deep greens.

"We need provisions," Eli said to Anna as they
passed a grocery store. "Stop here." The first time they'd
done this, after Mom left for rehab, felt like a million
years ago. So much had changed since Eli rolled around
the store on the cart, stopping for flowers and Doritos.

"How much did he give us?"

"Three hundred and fifty bucks."

"Okay, that's it, we both have to go to college so that we have three-fifty lying around the house just for, apparently, whatever. Like your daughter you don't know about and her kid sister showing up out of nowhere. And you're like, here, I went to college, have some chump change."

"Only stuff that won't go bad. The car smells bad enough with you in it."

Anna clearly didn't want any more college talk. She tossed a bag of Doritos into the cart. They picked up sandwich bread and peanut butter, plastic knives, three other kinds of chips, a case of soda, some beef jerky ("Protein," Anna said), donuts ("Breakfast," Eli said), and a few packs of Chips Ahoys and Oreos. Then they went to the deli counter and ordered sandwiches and sodas for lunch.

"How long do you think this will last us?" asked Eli.

"I don't have any idea, honestly," said Anna. "I guess we just have to do what your man Cliff says." Eli looked at her, confused. "You know, take it one day at a time?"

"Please shut up and pay," said Eli.

Back in the car, Anna started the engine but didn't drive.

"Tired?"

"Yeah. Also, Aunt Lisa . . ."

"Not up for meeting yet another long-lost relative today?"

"For real."

"Maybe we could find a motel?"

"I don't know, PB. Booking a room with a fake ID and a maxed out credit card?"

"You're Anna Banana. You'll make it work. Let's try to find one with a pool."

Motel on Rt. 3 was aptly named. The girls saw it down the road, with its flashing vacancy sign, "free cable" (why the quotes?), Wi-Fi, and, yes, a pool. Anna pulled over just before the entrance. She took out her makeup bag, cleanser and a cotton ball. Eli marveled at how she managed to bring all of this when Eli had barely managed an extra pair of underwear.

"Why are you taking it off?"

"Like you said, I'll figure it out. I'm figuring it out. Okay. Let's go. Look young."

Eli ruffled her own hair and put on a baseball cap. "Kid brother?"

"Let's do it."

The old woman at the desk eyed the two of them warily. Old women were a toss-up. They weren't usually going to fall for Anna's sexy tricks, but sometimes they could be charmed by Eli's adorableness. This was definitely going to be Eli's show.

"Good afternoon," Eli said. "Our mom wants us to get a room here for the night."

"Is that right, sonny?" The old woman's glasses hung on a chain around her neck. As long as she didn't use them, this routine might actually work.

"It is," started Anna. "She's out in the car with our new baby sister. She asked us to get things set up. Here's her license."

"A baby. I don't know about having a baby in here, all that crying . . ."

"Oh no," said Eli. "She hardly ever cries. I didn't either. Guess it runs in the family." She threw in a smile and an affable shrug for good measure.

"Is that right?" said the old woman, amused.

"We'd be happy to pay cash up front for the night, and if there's any problem, you hear her make one single peep, we'll get right on going." Anna's voice turned suddenly southern. She was trying too hard. She stopped speaking and held her breath.

"Deal."

The room had two queen beds with matching, slightly scratchy pink comforters that were made from anything but cotton. Eli and Anna threw themselves on the beds in relief. A ceiling fan swirled lazily above.

"Picnic by the pool?" Eli suggested, like this place was the Ritz.

"Sure." They didn't have bathing suits, but as Mom would say, that's what black underwear is for. Anna threw a T-shirt over a black bra and black underwear. Eli figured a pair of shorts and a sports bra were close enough. Sandwiches in hand, they headed down to the pool. The rickety stairs creaked. So did the beach chairs. It felt like paradise, sitting out under the sun with full bellies, the promise of more food later, and a place to sleep tonight. Eli inhaled deeply. She swore she could smell the ocean. It was probably just the sea salt and vinegar chips.

"Get in here!" Anna shouted as she jumped into the pool. The cold water splashed Eli's hot skin, and she dove in after her. "Handstand contest!" Anna declared as soon as Eli surfaced. Eli obliged immediately, despite knowing that she would lose. She came close, closer than she ever had before, but she toppled while Anna's legs were in the air, stock-still and unwavering. Somersaults came next, a contest Anna would also win, and then UnderwaterBob, which they were much too big to play now, but which had been Eli's favorite game when she was little. She would jump off Anna's knees into the water, and then they would both sit on the bottom of the pool pretending to be SpongeBob and Gary until they ran out of air. They both came up laughing.

The summer Anna was ten and Eli was six, Mom had brought them to the pool every day after work and on weekends. That was the good summer. Mom was better then, or at least, better than she was now. Eli's hair had turned even blonder in the sun, and she and Anna had both burned and tanned and burned and tanned. It was the happiest summer they'd ever had. Their happiest anything, maybe. Mom would get in the water with them, tossing them over her shoulders and racing them from one end to the other. That summer, they'd all smelled like sunscreen and chlorine all the time, even first thing in the morning or right after a shower.

"Do you remember that summer that we lived at the pool?" asked Eli.

"Oh, you mean Mom's sober summer. Yeah, I remember."

"She was sober?"

"The whole summer long. That's why she had so much energy, and why we had to be out of the house all the time. She was pacing the floors if she was stuck inside, but she was happy at the pool. So were you, SpongeBob."

"I remember."

Anna swam a lap down and back, splashing Eli by-accident-on-purpose when she turned.

"Why'd you do it?" Eli asked.

"Splash you? Because you're my sister and it's my god-given right to torture you."

"No, why did you disappear? Why didn't you come home for a week? I'm not even that mad anymore, I'm just . . . How could you do that to me? To us?"

Anna dunked her head underwater. "Honestly, Eli, I'm not sure I can explain it. And I'm not sure you'd understand it if I did."

"Try me."

"Do you ever feel like your entire life is just a series of things that happen to you? Like you're not actually living—you're just walking from one thing that happens to you to the next thing that happens to you and trying to survive in between?"

Eli nodded.

"Well, Jason made me feel alive. Like I had an actual life that was mine, and a body that was mine. The stuff with Peterson, this shitstorm with Mom, it all felt like it didn't matter. What mattered was that this guy who I had liked for an entire year knew me and liked me and chose me. And he brought me pancakes, and took me to the beach, and that was so much better than going to trigonometry, it didn't even feel like a decision. It just felt like fate. That sounds dumb. And selfish. It *is* dumb and selfish. But it felt good too."

"Better than being at home with your kid sister. I get it."

"Yes, and I hope you have times in your life too when something so powerful happens that it makes you lose all sense of perspective. I hope someone knocks you so far off your feet that you lose all that hard-won sense you've got. I hope they make you feel a million miles away and right there at the same time."

Eli's mouth drew tight. Meena. She closed her eyes.

"Or maybe someone already has. And so you know. And so maybe you can forgive me. I am sorry. I shouldn't have disappeared. It was just so tempting, so easy to think, this is my new life—my new life where I can feel like this all the time."

"Your new life without me in it."

"I don't have a life without you in it, Eli. Do you know what my earliest memory is? It's you. You were on the changing table, and the phone started to ring and Mom turned to get it, and I was so scared you'd pick that second to learn how to roll over, I stood on my tiptoes reaching my hands up to catch you if you fell. Your big, blond head just staring at me with this silly, drooly smile while I was basically saving your life. There's no me without you, kid."

"There isn't a me without you either. So you gave me six days without me."

"I know I did. I'm sorry. I wasn't trying to escape you, Eli. I was trying to escape me. And so I did the shitty, selfish, easy thing. I won't do it again."

"It was shitty and selfish. I hope you get to feel that way again, though."

"Me too."

"But I hope next time there's room for me too."

"There will be. So what happened? Who knocked your socks off? Who's making you feel this way?"

"Meena."

"It finally happened, huh? Good for you, kid."

"Good for me. Her dad walked in. She pushed me off her like I was a freak. I haven't talked to her since."

"Has she tried to talk to you?"

"She's texted and whatever."

"Has it occurred to you that she might have been freaked out by her dad, not by you?"

"Honestly, no."

"Well, that might be it, PB. Has Meena ever made you think that you're a freak before?"

"No."

"Then why would she now? Maybe you're the one who thinks you're a freak."

Eli felt her throat go lumpy and hard.

"Don't cry, little fool. Just call her. When, you know, we're not fugitives anymore."

"Speaking of fugitives, I have to tell you something."

"What?"

"You're not the only reason the social worker came. I mean, it's still mostly your fault. Just . . . not entirely. I got suspended."

"You? Miss Goody-Goody, friend of the principal's kid? What did you do?"

"I punched Kevin."

"Well, good for you. Come on, it's getting dark. We have to go check on Mom and the baby."

That night they piled all their food and clothes on one scratchy pink bed and curled up together on the other. They slept hard and long, smelling like salt and sun.

—17—

THEY LEFT THE next morning before the old woman could wake up from her desk and realize that it was just Anna and Eli after all. Eli was asleep, her head resting uncomfortably on her chest, when she felt the car suddenly swerve.

"What the hell?"

"Sorry, I just . . . I need to check something out."

"What is it?"

"I know this town."

Eli looked up. They were turning off the highway; the exit sign said Bristol in big, white letters.

"What's in Bristol?"

"That's what I'm trying to remember. Be quiet."

They rode along in silence. So far, Bristol looked just like any other town they'd been to, besides Fairview. Hills leading to valleys, houses leading to a McDonald's and a Home Depot, and a mall that was going out of business.

"Sam's mom lived here."

"Okay. You were, like, four—you really remember where she lived? I don't even know his last name."

"Collins."

"Oh." Eli reached into her backpack, thinking the word *Collins* over and over. Eli Collins, she thought before guilt shooed it away. "Anne Collins, 954 Edgewater Court, Apartment 4J, Bristol."

"Address book, huh?"

"That's what it says."

"Worth a shot."

"So, your long-lost dad turns out not to be a total asshole and now we have to go find mine?"

"Sam is the closest thing I had to a dad until yesterday. And his mom is nice. Don't be a jerk."

The apartments at Edgewater Court were brown and square and all the same. Eli and Anna walked up and down four different sets of buildings before they found 954. Anna knocked on the door. A hand quickly moved a curtain and then moved it back. Eli stiffened.

"Oh my god," the woman said as she opened the door, finally. "You're just his spitting image. You must be Sam's little girl."

Not really either one of those things, but okay, thought Eli.

"Um, yeah, my name is Eli. This is my sister, Anna."

"I remember pictures of you, Anna. You're all grown up now."

"I thought this was Sam's mom's house. I'm sorry—" started Anna.

"Mom died a few weeks ago; I'm just here cleaning up. I'm Sam's sister, Nicole. Come on in."

The apartment was dark and warm, a little like an old-lady cave—doilies covering every surface, floral patterns on everything from the wallpaper to the coasters.

"I'm sorry about your mom," said Eli.

"I met her a few times," Anna added. "She was really nice to me."

"She loved you both. How is your mom?"

"Fine," they said in unison.

"Sure," said Nicole, with a sunny voice but no smile. "Have a seat."

The girls sat on a yellow couch with tiny blue flowers, the plastic cover sticking to the backs of their bare legs.

"So, what brings you two by?"

"Um . . ." said Anna.

"I wanted to meet Sam," Eli covered. "I've heard so much about him, but I was just a baby when he left, and I don't remember him. I have these postcards." She took them out of her backpack.

"Oh, honey. These are sweet. He loved you two so much." The catch in Nicole's throat told Eli that bad news was coming. "Sam died shortly after this last one. He was in a car accident driving from Wisconsin to California."

A tear slid down Anna's cheek. Eli dug her nails into her palms and tried not to let out the gasp that was pushing its way out of her mouth.

Nicole offered a sad smile to both of them. "It's funny that you're here, actually. I just found this the other day. It's for you both. I didn't know how to find you or I would have sent it on." She rummaged through a stack of mail on the coffee table and handed them an unstamped envelope that just said "My Girls" on the front.

"Can I get you two something to eat?"

"No thanks," said Eli.

"Where's your mom?" Nicole asked.

Eli didn't like the way she put the emphasis on *where*, or the suspicious tone she gave to the word *mom*. "She's at home."

"Does she know you're here?"

Anna cracked her knuckles quickly.

"Yeah, she said it was okay," Eli replied.

"Well, you two make yourselves comfortable. I'll be right back."

Eli held a finger to her lips as she carefully removed herself from the plastic-covered couch. Nicole's brown purse hung from the back of the dining room chair a few feet away. Eli opened it.

"What the hell, Eli?" Anna whispered.

Eli held up her finger again and opened the snake-skin wallet. Coming from the back room, Nicole's voice was muffled but it was clear she was on the phone.

"Hi Janet, it's Nicole calling. I need to speak with a supervisor. Is anyone around?'

Eli pulled out a card from the wallet: Nicole Collins, MSW. Child and Family Services. She handed it to Anna, and then grabbed Anna's hand.

"We have to go. Now."

They ran out from the old-lady cave into the blinding light of day, down the stairs, past the four identical buildings, and into the car. They did not breathe or speak until Bristol was miles behind them, until the comforting anonymity of the interstate swallowed them whole.

"You getting the feeling that—"

"Our luck is rapidly running out?" finished Anna. "Yes."

—18—

THEY DECIDED THAT the parking lot of the highway diner three hours outside of Oxbridge, Vermont, was as good a place as any to read a dead man's letter. Two states away from Edgewater Court, and they could finally breathe normally. Fortified by French fries and shakes, the sun setting on the mountains around them, Eli turned the dome light on, opened the letter, and placed it on the dashboard between them so that they could read it together.

> *My girls,*
> *I don't know when you'll be reading this, how old you'll be, where in life you'll find yourselves. Has little Eliza joined the Peace Corps? Has my Anna*

gone to the Olympics yet? There's a lot I don't know about the two of you, and a lot you two might not know about me. But before we get into any of that, please know that every single second of your lives I've loved you and I always will.

Anna, you are fearless and kind. You have this big heart, though by now you probably keep it protected. I hope you can let it roam free. You are independent and joyful and sharp as a tack. Don't ever, ever let anyone take any of that from you. When you were three years old, you watched the big kids climbing to the top of the jungle gym and said you wanted to, too. I was scared. You were so small, but you looked at me with those serious blue eyes and said that there was nothing you couldn't do. I believed you. I hope you believe you too.

Eliza, you are sunshine with feet. You might be just a baby, but I would recognize you at ten, at thirty, at sixty. That big grin gives you away, the easy laugh, and the way you love so hard. You couldn't have been more than six months old, and I dropped a hammer on my foot while I was carrying you. I cried out, swore, and you threw your arms around my neck, and left slobber on my cheek, trying to give me a feel-better kiss. The world will teach you to hide your softness, but I know it will always be there. I hope you love it as much as I do. I also hope that you know that it's okay to have days when you are not sunshine. It's okay if sometimes you feel like throwing hammers.

So, if you're reading this, your question is likely: what happened? I don't know what answers you've made up for yourselves, but I bet they're wrong. Here's the truth: I've known since I was a little boy that I was gay. But being gay in Middletown in the nineties, in the family I came from, well, that just wasn't going to work. So, I wasn't. I dated women, I hated myself, I hid myself. Then I met your mother, and Anna, I met you. On our first date, we went to the playground. How romantic, right? But it was the closest to falling in love that I'd ever felt. I chased you around, pushed you on the swings, and you fell asleep on the picnic blanket between us, and for the first time in my life, I thought, I could be happy.

And we were. I convinced myself that I could do this. We could build this life together. But your mother, the smartest woman I know, was too smart for that. I had grown distant, only interested in you two, so I didn't have to confront myself. And she grew distant in her own way too. And then, *one night, she told me with tears in her eyes that she wanted more than anything in the world for me to be happy. And that she knew that happiness couldn't only come from being a father, that I had to be myself. I was shocked. I thought I'd done such a good job of hiding but your mom has a way of seeing you even when you don't want to be seen. We both knew that I couldn't be myself in Middletown, and so, with her help, I left. It was the worst thing I have ever done, the most shameful and the most hopeful. Maybe there was another way to do it, but we were nineteen when we met, twenty-one when I left. I can offer you only the most pathetic excuse in the world—we did the best we could. I don't dare ask for your forgiveness. I only want you to know that I love you, that I always have and that I always will. Being your father was the greatest honor I have ever had.*

    All my love,
    Sam

P.S. Should anything ever happen to me, there are savings accounts with each of your names on them. There won't be much, but I do hope this small act of fatherhood will remind you that I love you both, each and every day.

In the silence, Anna grabbed for Eli's hand. Eli squeezed back, and they sat there for a long, long time.

"It wasn't her fault," Anna said quietly.

"What?"

"It wasn't her fault. I have blamed her for Sam leaving every single day since I was five years old. It wasn't her fault." Anna's shoulders shook as she cried. Eli hugged her tight.

"It was nobody's fault," Eli said.

"He loved us," Anna said.

"A lot. And hey, here's some good news—looks like I really was born this way."

Anna laughed, and sniffed through her tears. "Yes, gaymo, it really does."

"You look like a raccoon," Eli said, and handed her some crumpled napkins from the glove compartment. Anna dabbed her eyes. Then she smiled her Anna Smile, all mischief and adventure.

"Want to learn how to drive?"

The car felt like a sailboat under Eli's hands, wobbly and easily toppled. Anna adjusted the mirrors for her. The floor rattled under her feet in a way she'd never felt in the passenger seat.

"Eli, it'll be easier if you put it in drive," Anna said, playfully annoyed. Eli exhaled. "Touch the gas, lightly."

Eli turned the world's slowest circle around the diner parking lot. "Okay." Anna laughed. "Not quite that lightly."

Fifteen slow circles later, Anna pointed Eli towards the highway.

"I can't," said Eli.

"You can. You must. One more circle and I'll hurl."

Eli did it. First, too slowly, weaving between lanes like a lost fish. It was hard to believe Anna when she said the secret was to drive faster, but once the speedometer hit sixty-five, Eli couldn't stop smiling. And she stopped weaving.

"It's good, right?" said Anna.

Eli nodded.

"Roll down your window."

The highway was empty; the stars shone above the streetlights. The warm night flowed in through the open windows, and they breathed in the start of summer. Anna stuck her hand out, feeling the wind push against it.

"Come on, try it," she yelled over the howl of the wind rushing into the car.

Eli did.

"Feels like you're flying, right?"

"Like I'm free," Eli yelled back.

—19—

ELI TOOK IT as a compliment to her excellent driving skills when Anna fell asleep on the road. After fields, mountains, woods, and long boring stretches of highway, she came to a stop in what she could only describe as "downtown" Oxbridge. Middletown was a small town, but this was different—Eli searched for the word, one no one would use to describe Middletown— it was cute. Anna stirred when Eli stopped at one of the three traffic lights.

"Where are we?"

"Oxbridge."

"Dude, I'm not sure I'm ready to deal with Aunt Lisa."

"Yeah, Banana, but how could we be ready? Have we been ready for any of this? Dead, gay Sam? Two rabid social workers? John? Meena? The Jacket? Mom in freaking rehab? There is no *ready* anymore."

"Do you remember Aunt Lisa, Eli?"

"I mean, kind of. Not really. She's tall."

"Yeah, she's tall. She gets in drunk fights with our mom and doesn't talk to her for years. The last time we saw her I was nine. I don't even think she'll know who we are. I'm just saying, I'm not sure about this."

"Me neither. But what else can we do?" Of course, at that moment, the gas light came on.

"Okay, screw it. Let's go." Anna looked around. "What is this place? It's so . . ."

"Cute, right?"

"Yeah. Switch seats with me."

Anna drove through downtown Oxbridge and it was objectively adorable—small shops, cottages in bright colors with impressive gardens, a river that whooshed under a wooden bridge, and up a hill, the ornate black-and-gold gates of Oxbridge College. Past the shops and the college, past everything, to where Oxbridge started to look a lot more like Middletown's outskirts, they saw a single beat-up apartment building, then trailers, then, well, nothing. Longmeadow Lane had neither a meadow nor a lane. What it did have was a long dirt road, twists and turns, and so many trees that Eli and Anna could no longer see the moon. Even with their brights on, they had to go slowly so they didn't drive off the "road." They missed the turn twice, until Eli spotted the tree with a 7 nailed into it. They were entirely too close to it when the outline of the dark cabin finally came into view against the dark sky.

"Stop!" Eli shouted. "You're going to hit her house!" Anna put the car in reverse but was stopped by a sharp tap of metal against metal.

"Stop is right," a low voice said sharply.

"Shit," Anna said. Eli squeezed her hand; it was as sweaty as her own. A hand appeared where Eli had rolled the window all the way down. A glint of something silver shone from the other hand.

"Well, hell," said the gruff voice. "You're Carrie's kids, aren't you?"

They both exhaled.

"You two scared the shit out of me. Now back up. You're crushing my begonias."

As Anna put the car in reverse, Eli whispered, "Is that a gun, Anna? Does she have a freaking gun?"

"Probably. I don't know what this backwoods hellhole is, but I'm not stopping."

There was the sharp tap of what was probably a gun against the trunk.

"Get out of the car."

Eli wasn't sure whether their lives would be more at risk by doing what she said or not doing what she said. "Can you put the gun away first?" she asked.

Aunt Lisa laughed—at least it sounded like a laugh, just one quick bark into the night air. "This is a shovel. You drove over it when you crashed into my garden."

Eli and Anna exchanged a quick shrug and opened their doors.

"Come on, then," Aunt Lisa said, leading them towards the dark cabin. They each stepped carefully up two logs to the front porch, "See there," she said, pointing to the far side of the porch where a rocking chair seemed to move by itself and more silver shone in the moonlight. "That's a gun."

Inside, the cabin smelled like the obvious things—wood, the woods—and also maybe a little sweeter than might be expected from shovel-and-gun-toting Aunt Lisa, like something had been baked here recently. The smell was the nicest part of this place. There was a wood-burning stove, a couch, a kitchen table, and a bookshelf, all of which seemed like this was not their first home.

Aunt Lisa ushered them over to the kitchen table. "Sit," she said. They looked at her in the light for the first time as she took some mason jars down from a plywood shelf nailed up over the sink. She poured them some water. She was tall, just like both of them remembered, with short brown curls heading every which way from the ears up. Her red plaid shirt had been thrown on over some long johns. Her gray sweatpants had traces of brown in the knees and green at the bottom. "Speak."

Eli and Anna looked at each other.

"Cut the crap, kids. What happened? Where's your mom?"

"She's fine."

"Let's try that again. You haven't seen me in six years. Let's not have the first thing out of your mouth be a lie."

"She's in rehab," Eli said.

Aunt Lisa nodded. "And you need a place to stay,"

Eli and Anna nodded.

"Fine. We'll work it out in the morning. For now, know this: I don't know what kind of trouble the two of you have gotten yourselves into, but it can't be good if you're coming to me for a rescue. So, we're going to have two rules here. Don't leave. Don't lie. If I get up in the morning and you two are gone, you're going to leave me with no choice but to call the cops and report unaccompanied minors. Are we clear?"

"Yes, ma'am," they both said, a word neither of them had uttered in their lives.

"Good. You'll sleep on the couch. It's not much, but it's what I've got." With that, she stood up, went over to the couch, and kicked out a leg so it folded down into a bed. She lay out some sheets and a blanket, pointed them in the direction of the bathroom. "If you hear scratching at the door, that's just Champ, my dog. Probably found a squirrel he wants to show me. Don't let him in unless you want squirrel blood all over your shoes. Good night."

Silently, Eli and Anna got ready for bed and turned out the light. Lying side by side on the itchy blanket on the too-small "bed," they took out their phones. Anna texted Eli, a smart move, so as to not wake Aunt Lisa or be overheard.

Wow, dude, great idea you had coming here.

What are we going to do?

What choice do we have? We'll stay here. We'll try not to get shot.

Okay. Let's also try not to get covered in squirrel blood. Do you think she's crazy?

Yes.

Do you think she's gay?

Duh. I guess at this point, in this family, I should be surprised I'm not.

Maybe you are, never know.

Ask Jason. I know.

Ew.

Go to sleep.

You first.

And then they rolled to their right, Eli on the inside, Anna curled around her. Just as they were starting to fall asleep, there was a scratch on the door, first one, then four, then another and a howl. Anna yelped in surprise.

"Don't worry, sister, it's just the sound of your shoes filling with squirrel blood. No big deal." And they both laughed until Anna put her hand over Eli's mouth, shushing her. "Okay, fine," Eli whispered. "I'll stop laughing." Her silent giggles turned into Anna's silent giggles, shaking the flimsy couch until they finally fell asleep.

"Which one of you is going to get the eggs?"

It was still dark when Eli and Anna opened their eyes to see Aunt Lisa standing over them.

"We're sleeping."

"I see that. My day starts at 4:45. I let you sleep until six. Now it's time to get up. There's no such thing as a free meal—you're going to want breakfast, so you're going to help get it. The chickens are in the back." With that, Aunt Lisa walked out the door.

"I can't believe this shit," Anna said, as she shook Eli. "Get up, PB. Apparently, we're late for work. Aunt Lisa's going to make us earn our keep. But oh my god, please first go brush your teeth."

With the sun rising through the trees, Longmeadow Lane was almost pretty. Eli and Anna stumbled out the front door, taking in the scene they'd created the night before. The car had left tracks in the dirt (well, in what used to be a flower garden) just inches away from the log walls of the cabin. Streaks of red, yellow, orange, and green ran from the edge of the house to the tires of the car, the petals separated from their flowers, heads separated from their stems, a sad row of lettuce with tire tracks down their flattened heads. They both stared at the damage with open mouths.

"Wow," said Anna.

"Shh," said Eli, pointing to Aunt Lisa, who she'd just noticed, sitting at the end of the porch in the rocking chair (where was the gun?) with her eyes closed, her hands resting palms up on her knees. They tiptoed off the porch, heading to the back. The smell of chicken poop in springtime can take your breath away. It falls over you like a blanket, in your ears, your eyes, your mouth until it's so all around you that you have no choice but to get used to it. You can't fight chicken poop, it will always win. Eli was learning this the hard way.

"What the hell is that smell?" Anna groaned, pulling her shirt up over her nose.

"Oh. My. God," said Eli, before shutting her mouth, trying to keep the smell out.

"You're short," said Anna, eyeing the light blue chicken coop in the back corner of the yard, "You go get the eggs."

"You're skinny," said Eli. "I'm sure you can fit."

"Fine, we'll just do it together. Baby."

They approached the wooden coop carefully and quickly, not wanting to go too close, but not wanting to spend any more time than absolutely necessary near the smell either. The wood creaked as Eli and Anna leaned against the peeling white-and-blue paint to reach inside. Anna moved her hand slowly forward. They both shrieked when the largest, whitest hen made direct eye contact with Anna, flapping her wings and lurching her beak towards Anna's hands. They yanked their hands out of the coop, bodies against the peeling paint, panting.

"What the hell? How is this our life?" asked Anna.

"She was going to take off your hand," said Eli.

"I know! Okay, you try this time."

"So she can take off my hand? Thanks a lot."

"Dude, it's facing the chicken or facing Aunt Lisa without eggs. I vote chicken."

"Fine." Eli took a deep breath. She turned around and reached back in. "Hey, beautiful," she heard herself say, as she picked up the eggs closest to the opening. "Thank you so much for letting me come in here this morning; you're so sweet, yes, you are," she crooned as she passed each warm egg quickly back to Anna, who had started a small basket for them in her shirt. "There you go, pretty," she whispered as she scooted her hand next to the hen. "Just these last two—OW." Eli pulled her hand out with one last egg.

"You okay?" Anna asked.

Eli tossed her egg into Anna's shirt. "Yeah," Eli said, smiling, just a little proud.

"What other secret lives do you have, Farmer Eli?"

Eli looked at her own hands, just as surprised by her hen-handling skills.

"Seriously, how did you know how to do that?"

"Seriously, I have no idea."

They wandered into the kitchen looking for a place to set down their egg trove.

"Not bad," Aunt Lisa said, pouring a cup of coffee. "Too bad about your shirt, Anna." She handed them a bowl for the eggs. When Anna's shirt was egg-free, she discovered it was not free of chicken poop and feathers, which had left green and white stains from the collar to the hem.

"Shit!" she said as she stormed off to the bathroom.

Aunt Lisa made that half-laugh, half-bark noise again. Eli began to make the bed back into a sofa. She just wanted something to do with her hands, which had started to sweat. Aunt Lisa made her nervous—the woman might be her aunt, but she was basically a total stranger.

"No one taught you how to fold a sheet, huh?" Aunt Lisa eyed the crumpled white ball, Eli's attempt at a square.

"Sorry," Eli said, embarrassed.

Aunt Lisa snapped the sheet out, flowing into the middle of the cabin with her outstretched arms. She looked oddly graceful, almost like a ballerina. Well, a ballerina with a camo jacket on. "Anna, come eat."

Anna came out of the bathroom wearing a new (identical) black T-shirt and holding the egg-mess shirt in her hand. "Where's the washing machine?"

"I'll get it out for you."

Anna and Eli exchanged confused looks as Aunt Lisa opened a closet and dragged a large metal box towards the kitchen sink. She linked a hose to the faucet and motioned for Anna's shirt. "While we're at it, why don't you guys put in the rest of what you've got. Smells like you've been on the road for a while."

Something in the way she said it, no judgment, just facts, let Eli know she wasn't being rude—and she wasn't wrong. It had been a while since they'd been in close proximity to a washing machine.

"When it's done running, you can hang your stuff up on the clothesline out back."

"You don't have a dryer?" asked Anna. All the judgment missing from Aunt Lisa's comment was dripping off hers.

"Nope, I think you'll find a few things here are different than what you're used to. Why don't you all sit down."

"No shit they're different," Anna said, pulling a wobbly wooden chair back from the kitchen table. "Like the 1800s were different."

"Sit."

Eli thought Aunt Lisa would be mad at Anna, but it seemed like she hadn't even heard what Anna said. She must be focused on getting ready to grill them.

"How long has your mother been in rehab?"

Here it comes, the barrage of awful questions, the prying loose of every detail, every lie, every misstep.

"Seventy-four days."

Aunt Lisa's right eyebrow arched slightly.

"Okay. She's got, what, sixteen to go?"

"Yeah," said Anna, her own eyebrow arching right back at her.

How did she know?

"All right, then." Aunt Lisa took a deep breath. "Days start at six. You're in charge of breakfast; I'll handle coffee. I work at the college in town. During the day, you'll do your schoolwork, and you'll rebuild the garden you drove into. Four nights a week, I go to AA meetings in town. There's Alateen meetings across the hall. You'll go to those."

"Oh my god, you're a drunk too? What luck."

"Bet your ass. Sober three years. You might not like the rules, but unless you've got some other long-lost aunt whose doorstep you can show up on, I say take 'em or leave 'em."

Anna took a sip of coffee and looked down.

Aunt Lisa got up from the table. "Clothespins are in the cabinet by the back door." She walked out the front door. Soon, they could hear the whoosh of an ax through the air and the sound of wood splitting open. Champ barked at a squirrel.

That afternoon, Eli knew it was time. She had to face Javi and Meena. She walked to the farthest corner of the backyard, away from the coop, near where her shirts blew in the breeze, starting to smell like sunshine. She could feel the sweat forming at her temples as she FaceTimed Javi first. The dull tone beeped once, twice, three times—was he ever going to pick up?

"Salve, puella." His face came into focus, his curls and kind eyes.

"Hi!"

"Hi. So, you're not dead."

"I'm sorry. I'm sorry I couldn't call earlier. It's complicated."

"Sure," he sounded unconvinced. "I've got some-one else here too." Meena's face came into the frame. She'd cut her hair. It was short in the back and came to asymmetrical points at her chin. The room went a little spinny, like just for a second Eli could feel Earth mov-ing around the sun.

"Hey," Meena said.

"Hey."

"Are you okay? Where are you?"

"I'm in Vermont. I am okay. I'm really sorry, guys."

"We're listening," said Javi.

"I don't even know where to start."

"Why don't you try the truth? Seems like we haven't been getting a lot of that from you lately."

"I haven't lied to you guys."

"Telling us nothing about your life and acting like we're your friends is a kind of lying, E." Javi again. Looking down. Like he barely wanted to talk to her.

"Okay. Well, about two months ago my mom went to rehab. I didn't tell you because I couldn't tell you. We didn't have anyone else to stay with so my sister pretended to be my aunt so that we wouldn't end up in foster care. We couldn't tell anyone because we couldn't risk getting separated. That's why I've been so weird lately. I mean, among other things."

She tried to just look at the phone, to not look at Meena so that the world would stay on its axis. "We'd been doing okay. But then my sister got this boyfriend and didn't go to school for, like, a week. And then I punched Kevin and got suspended. And they weren't going to let me come back to school without a parent-teacher conference, and your mom isn't an idiot, Javi—she wasn't going to believe that my sister was my mom or even my aunt. And then my sister not going to school meant that they needed to talk to a parent, and since they couldn't reach one for a week, they sent a social worker over to see what was going on. So we had to leave."

"What did you do?"

"We climbed out the back window and down the fire escape and sped off. We got to my aunt's house yesterday. She lives in Vermont. She says we can stay with her until my mom gets out of rehab."

"When's that?" asked Meena.

"Two more weeks."

"I'm glad you're okay," said Meena. "We miss you."

"We do miss you," said Javi. "And I'm sorry that this has been so hard, Eli, but you made it about a hundred times harder. Why didn't you tell me what was going on? I could have helped."

"I didn't want to put you in a bad spot with your mom. And I couldn't risk her telling Social Services what was going on, and she would have had to."

"Wow, way to trust me, Eli. I don't know what I did to make you think I would have run and told my mother. You're just like everyone else—you just think of me as the principal's son. It's like you're so busy 'protecting' me, you don't even give me a chance to be a good friend to you. Like you don't even notice the kind of friend I am. Well, newsflash, Eli, I'm the kind of friend who helped you, who cared about you, and who was there for you. But you were too busy lying to me to care." He turned to Meena. "I'm done, girl. Find me when you're finished with this."

Eli watched him get up, heard him close the door to his room *hard*. Meena's face filled the screen, alone.

"He's been really worried, Eli. We both have."

Eli closed her eyes to keep in the tears. It didn't work. "I'm sorry."

"When are you coming home?"

"When my mom gets out, two weeks from now."

"He might be mad, Eli, but we miss you. Don't do this again, okay?"

Eli nodded.

"I can't wait for you to come home."

Eli looked up long enough to see Meena's smile, the one that made her stomach flip. Meena was about to say something, but Eli could hear Javi calling from the other room.

"I've got to go," Meena said.

So all Eli said was "Bye."

—20—

LIKE CHICKEN POOP, Aunt Lisa was also always going to win. When she woke them at six to get eggs, she informed them that they would be calling their schools that day.

Anna said, "Like hell I will," and, "What does it even matter anyway?" and more Anna-like things, and Aunt Lisa said, in what could only be described as a growl, "I'm not watching one more smart woman in this family throw away her future," and she pushed open the front door and told Eli and Anna to get in the truck.

That was how they'd ended up in the bed of this beat-up red truck, trying to hold on down the bumps and turns of Longmeadow Lane until they got to Oxbridge. A blue-and-white sign announced that you were entering the campus, but it was unnecessary. This place was unmistakable. It looked like a movie set of a college, all rolling green lawns and big brick buildings with turrets—*turrets!* Like they were castles instead of classrooms. Aunt Lisa parked and they walked down wide, clean sidewalks past large, white houses, rocking chairs on wraparound porches, laughter coming from inside.

"Who lives here?" Eli asked.

"The students, these are dorms."

Eli was taking in everything—the girl with the neck tattoo walking a few feet in front of them, the boy in a kilt and army boots playing his guitar on the lawn, the smell of waffles somewhere.

"This is college, huh? You work here? Are you a professor?"

Aunt Lisa bark-laughed. "No, kid. I dropped out of high school in tenth grade when your mom left. I do shipping and receiving in the school bookstore. It's not a bad gig, and it means I get to go to school for free."

"This is like Hogwarts," Eli whispered.

"Not really," said Aunt Lisa. They walked up the slate steps of another castle-looking building, this one full of students and smelling like coffee.

"I thought you said you worked in the bookstore? Why does it smell like breakfast?"

"The bookstore is part of the student center. Come on, it's this way."

"Eli, Anna, this is Iris, Evelyn, and Beverly. Everyone, these are my nieces. They're visiting." Aunt Lisa didn't stop for them to do more than wave, and Iris, Evelyn, and Beverly barely looked up from their registers. Eli knew instantly they would never, ever be able to tell the women apart anyway. Aunt Lisa took them to meet Rita, the manager, but she was on the phone in her office. She waved at Aunt Lisa and tilted her head to the side when she saw Eli and Anna but decided whatever she was looking at on her computer screen was more important.

The bookstore itself was bright, with comfortable armchairs and every imaginable item with the word *Oxbridge* on it for sale. Sweatshirts, onesies, keychains, postcards, phone chargers, pens, Band-Aids, Post-its, cookies, water bottles. Like a convenience store that only sold one brand: Oxbridge. And then there were the books—rows of fiction, nonfiction, poetry, and then shelves lining the entire store and filled with textbooks laid on their sides. Between two shelves was a door that led to a dark hallway, down some back stairs, and into a basement.

"This is it," Aunt Lisa said as she hung her jacket on the back of her chair. She turned on a lamp by her desk and hit a button, which started the conveyer belt behind her.

"This is what?" said Anna.

"This is where I work, and where you two will be helping me today, and here is the phone from which we will call your schools."

"Can't we go sit upstairs?"

"Paying customers only. You got cash? Didn't think so. Now pass me a box cutter."

Aunt Lisa showed them where to get the boxes, and how to use a dolly to load them up and bring them in. She scanned the boxes and Eli sent them up the conveyor belt to go out on the floor.

"After lunch, we'll shelve what we've sent up."

"Fun," said Anna.

"No one said it was fun. You want fun, stop wasting that brain and go to college."

Anna walked back to load more boxes from the truck that had conveniently arrived.

"She never wants to talk about college," Eli said. Aunt Lisa just gave a sigh as she lifted a box onto the belt.

Aunt Lisa let them out of the dungeon, as Anna called it, to have lunch. "Go eat, then we're calling your schools. Don't wander."

Anna and Eli waited on lines in the student center for different forms of fried food. They went outside to watch the students walk by, Anna trying to look cool and unimpressed, Eli openly gaping.

Aunt Lisa's shadow appeared over them minutes later. "Okay, guys. We have some phone calls to make."

Eli noticed that Aunt Lisa always said "guys" instead of "girls." She liked that.

"Who's first?" Neither of them spoke. "Okay, Anna, let's go."

Eli could see Anna beginning to say, "Why me?" before she shut her mouth, gave up, and followed Aunt Lisa back inside.

Eli waited, the pit in her stomach growing bigger. She should have gone first. She distracted herself, watching the college kids come and go, a blur of backpacks and skateboards and bicycles and earbuds. A couple walked by holding hands, one with half her head shaved, her dark hair parted on the side and tucked behind her multiply pierced ear. The other one had short blond hair, shorter than Eli's, peeking from under a backwards baseball cap, and wore old Vans and ripped jeans, and carried a skateboard covered in stickers. Eli couldn't take her eyes off the two of them. She wanted that. That cool, easy, just a regular Wednesday vibe. A girl's hand in hers, walking around, unbothered, practically unnoticed.

She couldn't tell if the blond was a boy or a girl, and she liked it that way. Sometimes it gave Eli a little bit of a thrill when people guessed her gender wrong. Not like Kevin, who asked her if she was a boy or a girl when he damn well knew the answer, but there was a power in confusing people, and to not giving a shit, and this couple looked very powerful for a Wednesday morning.

Anna plopped down next to her.

"How did it go?" Eli asked, forgetting the happy couple.

"Not as bad as it could have, I guess."

Aunt Lisa's voice boomed over them; Eli hadn't realized she'd followed Anna back out.

"They're letting you go into twelfth grade, if you finish the rest of your work for the year, and pass your finals. You're lucky. The world doesn't owe you a living just because your home life is on fire."

"Harsh," said Anna, sucking soda through her straw even though it was empty.

"Eli, you're up," Aunt Lisa said.

They went back down to the basement, sunshine and grass lawns and cute couples with skateboards seemingly miles away.

"What are you waiting for? Dial."

"Aren't you the one who's calling?" Eli asked.

"It's *your* life, Eli. Not mine."

Eli nodded. Aunt Lisa put the phone on speaker and let the dial tone blare out awkwardly until Eli started to punch in the numbers. Mrs. Johnson answered with her usual warm, nasal voice as she said, "Just a minute, sweetie." She called everyone sweetie; it never even seemed condescending since she was about eight hundred years old. Eli could hear the familiar noise in the background—the slamming of doors, the laughter, the ringing bells, the ringing phones, someone asking for a late pass.

"Hello, this is Principal Calderón," Eli could see her now, her black hair pulled into a bun that was always threatening to come undone, the smile that didn't appear that often, but took up her entire face when it did. She had given that smile to Eli more than once.

"Um, hi, this is Eli. Eli Reynolds."

"Oh, Eli, I'm happy to hear from you. Are you okay? We miss you around here."

"I'm okay. Um, I'm sorry about punching Kevin."

"That's pretty much the least of our worries right now, Eli. Where are you?"

"I'm with my aunt in Vermont."

"Hi there, my name is Lisa Reynolds," Aunt Lisa chimed in, all of her gruffness smoothed out, sounding like a Hallmark commercial's idea of an aunt. "I'm the kids' guardian while their mom is in rehab."

"Okay," said Principal Calderón, surprised. "That's good to know."

"Um, yeah. So, that's why my mom didn't come in after my suspension."

"I understand. I wish you had said something. You've had us all so worried."

"I know. But I didn't want to be separated from my sister. When the social worker came to our place, we took off and went to our aunt's house," Eli said, skipping a few details. "We want to stay here until my mom gets out of rehab. But I know that means missing a lot more school."

"How much longer will your mom be away, Eli?"

"About two weeks."

"Okay. So, that puts you back here for the last week of the year, more or less. I'll talk to your teachers. Lisa, is there somewhere we could send work for Eli?"

"Absolutely, Eli and her sister are working at my office trying to catch up on schoolwork. If you give me an email address, I'll write you for it today."

"Great. I'll put this in as a leave of absence, and it'll end in two weeks. You'll be responsible for the work you miss during that time, and the work you've missed since last week. Understood?"

"Yes. Thank you."

"You're welcome. Eli?"

"Yes."

"You scared Javi. You scared all of us."

"I know. I'm sorry."

"He loves you, Eli. You matter to him. To us. I don't think you really understand that. Maybe you'll use these next two weeks to think about that a little."

"Okay."

"Okay. Thank you again, Lisa. We'll be in touch with work."

"Thank you."

Aunt Lisa got Principal Calderón's email and ended the call. The room went silent. "You okay, kid?"

Eli wanted to answer, wanted to look up confidently and say, "Yeah, I've got this!" but there were tears all over her face. Aunt Lisa put a hand awkwardly on Eli's shoulder. Took it off. Put it back on. "Let's go get the rest of your fries before your sister eats them."

That night at dinner, Aunt Lisa told them they weren't done with the phone calls.

"When was the last time either of you spoke to your mother?" They looked at each other, and then at their respective plates of spaghetti. "Well, it's time."

"I don't want to talk to her," said Anna.

"Join the club," said Aunt Lisa. "Unfortunately for you, she's your mother, and she has a right to know where you are. I can't just keep you here."

"Why not?" Eli asked.

Aunt Lisa sighed. "Because it's not my call. She's your mom. Like it or don't. She's your mom and she needs to know where you are."

"Half the time she doesn't even know where *she* is," Anna said. "And how worried can she be? She didn't worry about us when she was leaving me in charge of Eli and an apartment she had no way to pay for."

"You really don't understand this thing, do you?"

"Blah, blah, blah, it's a disease. I know. Please don't make excuses for her."

"You're right." Eli and Anna looked up. This was the last thing they expected to hear. "You are, you're right. This sucks. You shouldn't be here, you should be hanging out with your friends, doing homework, messing up, making little mistakes with little consequences. You deserve a safe home, you deserve a responsible parent. It sucks that you don't have one, and it sucks that she's put you through hell. And someday we'll figure all that out. But that's not tonight. Tonight you're going to let the woman who gave birth to both of you know that you're alive."

Anna and Eli both rolled their eyes. Aunt Lisa picked up her phone.

"Green Hills Wellness Center, how may I direct your call?"

"My name is Lisa Reynolds. I need to speak with Carrie Reynolds; she's a patient."

"One moment." The wait felt endless. Tinny hold music played from Aunt Lisa's phone. Eli poked her meatball around her plate. Anna elbowed her to stop.

"Hello?"

"Carrie? Hi, it's Lisa. I'm sorry to be calling, but I've got Anna and Eli here." She nodded, forcefully, at both of them.

"Hi, Mom," they said in unison.

"My babies!"

Eli could hear tears in her voice already.

"What are you doing in Vermont? Are you okay?"

"We're okay," they said.

"They've gotten themselves in some scrapes but they've got your brains, Carrie; they're okay," Aunt Lisa chimed in.

"What happened?"

Eli and Anna looked at each other, and then to Aunt Lisa. She nodded.

"A social worker came by the house so we had to leave," said Anna.

"Why did a social worker come?"

"Because, Mom, we're two teenagers living by ourselves, pretending to be Aunt Lisa and her ward. Did you think no one was going to notice?" She looked at Aunt Lisa who nodded again. "And also because I didn't go to school for a few days and Eli got into a fight."

"You weren't in school? What were you doing? You know you need to take care of your sister. Eli, are you okay?"

"I'm fine, Mom. I threw a punch, like you taught me. I got suspended and they needed a parent-teacher conference for me to come back to school, so I didn't go back."

"And Anna, where the hell were you?"

"I swear to God, Mom, I don't know how you can possibly judge—"

"Carrie—"

"Save it, Lisa," Mom said, taking a breath. "I know they're right." She sounded defeated. "I know this is a bad situation, and I know you are both doing the best you can. And Anna, you know I think you take great care of Eli."

"Who is not six and doesn't need that much taking care of," said Eli.

"True. But you two are wonderful sisters to each other, and I'm very grateful for that. When you didn't show up last weekend, I got worried, that's all. It's hard being far from you, and so, so powerless to help or to take care of you." Last weekend, Family Day. Anna and Eli's jaws dropped. They'd completely forgotten.

"We are so sorry we missed it, Mom," said Eli.

"Yeah," said Anna slowly.

"It's okay. I'm just glad you're okay. I thought maybe you were too angry to come, which would have been okay too. But I'm glad it's not that."

"It's not that," Anna finally said.

"These are some really smart kids you've got," Aunt Lisa said.

Eli and Anna looked at each other. Was she just being nice?

"They take good care of each other. We'll come pick you up in two weeks."

"All of you?'

"If that's okay."

"I'd like it." Mom's voice sounded like a child's— soft, high, hopeful.

"We'll see you soon."

"We love you," said Eli.

"I love you too." And they hung up.

—21—

CHURCH BASEMENTS ALL smell the same—
old and cold. Eli felt bad for Aunt Lisa, having to spend
so much of her time in them. But every Monday, Thursday, Friday, and Sunday, there she was. She brought Eli
and Anna with her early to help make coffee and set
up chairs.

"Why are we doing this?" Anna asked.

"Because it keeps me sober."

"How does it keep *you* sober for *me* to set up
chairs?"

Aunt Lisa laughed once. "Setup keeps me sober.
I volunteer to do it because it means I have to come
even when I don't want to. You're just here because I
said so."

Anna smirked and unfolded another chair. "Well, I don't get it."

"And I hope you never have to."

People had started filing in, laughing and talking and filling Styrofoam cups with coffee that looked more like muddy water than coffee.

A young woman with black hair that came to severe points at her chin, black lobe expanders in her ears, and a black hoodie came up to Aunt Lisa. She looked like she would as soon snarl as say hi, but she leaned into Aunt Lisa for a hug.

"Check out Aunt Lisa's girlfriend," Anna whispered to Eli.

"Guys, this is Lacey, my sponsee."

Eli elbowed Anna, *Not girlfriend*.

"Nice to meet you." Lacey's smile changed her whole face. "You're lucky to have an aunt like Lisa. She's saved my ass, that's for sure. But I guess that's what sponsors are for." It was weird to hear someone talk about Aunt Lisa with so much admiration in her voice. Eli and Anna mostly talked about her with confusion at best, and maybe some fear.

"What's a sponsor?" Eli asked.

Aunt Lisa answered, "Someone who helps you get sober, like my sponsor helped me."

"Who's your sponsor?"

"Jane. She's over there." Jane looked like some-body's grandmother, complete with neat bun and old-lady glasses. It was hard to imagine her doing anything more reckless than playing bingo. It was hard to imagine Aunt Lisa looking to her for a hug, hard to imagine Aunt Lisa being as shaky and grateful as Lacey.

Next to Jane, getting coffee, was Rita from the bookstore. She saw them seeing her and came over. This night was weird and getting weirder.

"You're Lisa's nieces. I'm Rita. Getting used to Oxbridge?"

"Um, yeah, it's cool," managed Eli, glancing at Anna to say, *What is happening?*

"Erica!" Rita called across the hall. A girl with long curly hair and glasses came over. She was wearing a blue Oxbridge High School varsity wrestling sweatshirt. "This is my daughter, Erica. She's a senior at Oxbridge High. She'll be at the Alateen meeting across the hall."

"Hey," she said, offering her hand.

"Hey," Eli and Anna said back.

"Sorry," said Anna. "This is a little . . ."

"Weird?" Erica asked. "You bet. It's super weird. The weirdest part is that it helps. Come meet the other weirdos."

Across the hall in a nearly identical room were ten chairs set up in a nearly identical circle. On the side, there was a table with cookies instead of coffee. A handful of other kids milled around, talking and chewing. An older woman with graying blond hair was already sitting in the circle.

"Guys, this is Eli and Anna. They're new." Everyone waved and smiled and continued chatting. "That's Eileen; she runs the group," Erica gestured to the seated woman. Someone asked Erica a question—Eli was relieved to have the attention off of them.

"Could this be weirder?" Eli asked.

"I mean, it hasn't even started yet, so I'm sure it'll get weirder," Anna said.

As if on cue, Eileen said, "All right, everyone, let's get started. I've asked a friend to read the preamble."

"Hi, I'm Anthony," said a boy quietly, as his dark hair fell into his face, covering his dark eyes.

"Hi Anthony!" the entire group said in unison.

Weirder, mouthed Anna to Eli.

He read something in his quick, quiet voice, and then everyone started "sharing."

"Hi, I'm Lou," said a girl with pink pigtails and an eyebrow ring.

"Hi Lou," said everyone, as Eli rolled her eyes at Anna.

"I'm still working on forgiving my father. He died of this disease two years ago. I can't shake the feeling that he chose booze over me. I know that's not how it works. I know that no one chooses alcoholism. But it still sucks, and I'm still mad and I still miss him and I'm still mad that I miss him. I guess the key to it is acceptance, right? I can have more than one feeling at a time, even if I wish I didn't have any. Thanks for letting me share."

"Thanks," said the group. Anna stuck her hands in her hoodie pockets, and Eli looked at the floor.

"Hi, I'm Teddy," said a boy who looked like a football player, like a cartoon drawing of an all-American boy. Like he was born with a football in one hand and a piece of apple pie in the other. He reminded Eli of Kevin. She froze her face in a scowl.

"Hi Teddy."

"I don't know what to say. I've only been coming here for a little while. Maybe it's helping? My mom got out of rehab a month ago. She's doing okay, I guess. She's going to meetings. She seems so distracted, though, and she has such a short fuse. Here, I feel like I'm learning how to 'keep the focus on myself' or whatever that dumb expression is. I'm trying to see that whether or not she's sober doesn't determine *my* life. When she was drinking, my life was completely chaotic, full of the fights over nothing she'd have with my dad, and worrying about why she wasn't coming home. I taught myself to drive when I was twelve years old, just so I'd be able to get her from the bar if I had to. I learned all the rooms in the house that look out onto the driveway so that I could know the second she got home, and see from how she was driving what kind of state she was in. It was like a full-time job. Now, it's less chaotic, and that's good—I'm definitely happy she's sober. But it's not like it's suddenly perfect. She's still her, and she's still tired and moody and, I guess, human? But I've spent so much time focused on her, I don't even know what to do with myself. Guess I'll keep coming here and see if I can figure it out. Thanks."

"Thanks, Teddy."

Eli barely heard the next share, her head filled with the stories Teddy had told, the way they brought her stories along with them, the little glimpse of the not-entirely-sunny future he'd given.

"Hi, I'm Erica," Rita's daughter started to share.

"Hi Erica."

"So, my twin sister just got home from rehab. It's a lot. Like, how many people in my family can this thing hit? It's all anyone wants to talk about at school—half of them want to tell me how cool they think she is, and the other half are taking bets on how long it'll last this time. I want to tell all of them to go to hell. But I also wonder, you know, if it'll last. It's lasting for my mom so far, I guess. She's been sober a long time now.

But I don't know what will happen with Michelle. And what about me? Is it going to get me too? I feel like my sister and I had opposite reactions to my mom's alcoholism, like, Michelle was like, screw it, let's go, and I'm standing on the sidelines, scared of what one beer might do to me. But we've both got the other stuff—you know, always being on guard, not trusting new people, lying. It's hard to unlearn that, no matter how long my mom has been sober. But it is getting easier. You know. One day at a blah-blah-blah . . ." Everyone laughed. "Anyway. Thanks for letting me share."

"We have time," said Eileen. "Do either of our visitors want to share?"

Eli and Anna both shook their heads no.

"Actually, you know what, screw it," said Anna. "I'm Anna."

"Hi Anna."

"This is all really, really, really weird. But then again, my whole freaking life is weird right now. Our mom is in rehab, and we're staying in this tiny-ass town with an aunt we've met like once in our lives. I just want things to go back to normal, but I don't even know what that is anymore. It's sure as hell not this." Everyone waited. "Um. That's it."

Eli thought for sure they'd ask them to leave. Anna and her big mouth, always getting them in trouble.

"Thanks for sharing, Anna. We have a nice way of closing . . ."

Like they were all in a choreographed dance, everyone stood up and spread out their arms, joining hands, reaching out for Anna's and for Eli's too.

After a prayer that everyone said in creepy unison, everyone dropped hands. It was like they morphed into regular kids again, talking and laughing and eating more snacks. Pink pigtails came up to Anna and Eli.

"Hey, I'm Lou. Nice to meet you guys."

"You too."

"I'm sorry about your dad," Eli said.

"That's okay, thanks," said Lou. "Listen, I know this place is super weird. But if you guys are here, it's probably not because things are awesome. I hated it at first—we all do. But it starts to suck less; then it starts to help. I hope you come back."

"We don't exactly have a choice," said Anna. "Our aunt is one of the drunks across the hall. She's making us come as long as we're staying with her."

"Ah, yes. Bold move. Well, we'll see you tomorrow then."

"Hey, little man," said Teddy, offering Eli a pound. For some reason, Eli didn't correct him.

"Hey," she said. "I'm Eli."

"Good to meet you. Sorry about your mom."

"It's okay; it's probably for the best. It helped your mom, right?"

"Yeah. It's hard at first. I basically had to finally be angry at her after just being worried for fifteen years straight. When I was worried, I couldn't let myself be angry. Now, I know she can handle it."

Eli stared into his face. How could this total stranger know everything about her? Why was this boy telling her all of this, and why did that feel so good?

"Yo, Anthony, can I get a ride? Gotta go man—see you tomorrow?"

"See you," she said, stunned.

There was loud laughter from across the hall, applause, and the sound of fifteen folding chairs scraping against the floor simultaneously.

Erica appeared beside Eli and Anna in the hall. "Well, you made it through your first meeting."

They both nodded.

"It gets less weird."

"That's what I'm afraid of," said Anna.

"Anna, don't be rude," said Eli.

"It's not rude for her to say what she's thinking. And don't worry, I'm not so easily offended. I felt the same way when I first came here. But my family felt so screwed up, I needed someplace to talk about it. Now that I can talk about it, it feels a little less screwed up.

Or, at least, I do. Anyway, a bunch of us go bowling after the meeting on Friday. You should come."

"Maybe," said Anna.

"Oh, I know. It's a hopping town, lots of options to choose from," Erica said with a smile.

Before they went to sleep that night, Anna leaned on one arm in bed.

"To be clear," she said. "We are not bowling with those freaks."

—22—

THE BOOKSTORE WAS closed on Friday for finals, and Aunt Lisa took her day off to make a lunch of roasted rabbit and kale from the garden. As Eli tried very hard not to think of Thumper, Bugs, Peter, The Easter Bunny or even the Energizer Bunny, Anna asked Aunt Lisa why she didn't have a TV.

"Is this some kind of sober thing? Beer ads or something?"

"No, it's not. Sober people can watch TV. But between taking care of this land, going to work, going to class, and going to meetings, I don't have a lot of kick-back-and-watch-cartoons time."

"Wow. You really want to go to college that badly?"

"Yup," she paused. "You should too."

"College? I don't know. It seems hard."

"You're a lot of things, Anna, but a chicken isn't one of them. And college isn't nearly as hard as not going to college."

"We'll see. So, what do you do for fun, then? Like, do you have any?" You could always count on Anna to change the subject back to anything else when someone asked her about college.

"I like to hunt, hence the gun you thought I was going to shoot you with. And you can spare the judgment—I only kill to eat. I used to like my garden before some punk teenagers drove a beat-up Honda through it." She smiled. It was the first time Eli thought Aunt Lisa maybe, maybe didn't hate the fact that her nieces had taken up residence on her couch.

"Yeah, okay, but like, for fun? Not for sustenance?"

Aunt Lisa shook her head from side to side and took a deep breath. "Honestly, I like jigsaw puzzles."

"Wow," said Anna.

"That's what you do . . . for fun?" said Eli.

"Listen, people. Puzzles are the best way to make the world right when everything is wrong. You two could probably use a puzzle." She got up from the table and went over to the big, blue cabinet in the corner of the living room. They watched her quizzically. She opened the doors to reveal neatly stacked puzzles piled on top of each other, more than sixty in all. She looked like a little kid farmer standing next to her prize pony.

"You want to try one? I've got one of fierce historical women, space, Broadway, best novels of the nineteenth century, *Peanuts*—you know, Charlie Brown, dogs, and a few gradient puzzles, but you aren't ready for that yet."

Eli and Anna looked at her and laughed. Aunt Lisa had never spoken this much, this quickly, this happily.

"Sure," they said in unison.

"Fierce historical women it is," said Aunt Lisa, pulling a box from the shelf. Eli and Anna cleared the table as Aunt Lisa set up. They gathered back around the table and Aunt Lisa split them up. Anna would look for Zora Neale Hurston, Adrienne Rich, and Sojourner Truth. Eli would look for Audre Lorde, Sor Juana, and Elizabeth Cady Stanton.

"I got this as a present for myself when I passed my gender studies final last year. I'll tell you a little bit about each of them, if you want."

Anna and Eli looked at each other, looked at Aunt Lisa, and started to laugh again.

"How about some music?" said Anna.

"Sure," said Aunt Lisa. "The radio is over there."

The only stations they could get out in the boonies were the country station and the classical station. They switched between the two for the rest of the day. They didn't finish until dinner, Hank Williams Jr. having given way to Hank Williams Sr. and then to Beethoven and finally to Dolly Parton, and the sisters smiling at each other with wide eyes as Aunt Lisa forgot about her audience and tough exterior and sang along quietly to "I Will Always Love You." Eli grabbed the last piece out of Anna's hands, and as promised, just for that moment, the world was made right.

"Which one of you wants to learn how to make coffee?" Aunt Lisa asked that night as she pulled the silver-and-black urn out of the cabinet built into the gray walls of the church basement.

"I know how," said Anna.

"You know how to press a button. I'm talking about industrial-sized coffee."

Eli wandered over; Anna did too. Eli scooped and scooped the grounds; Anna poured water up to the mark made on the inside by people brewing coffee in this same pot every night for years on end.

"Hey Anna, hey Eli," said Lou, poking her head around in from the doorway.

"Hi," they said.

"Glad guys you came back."

They both smiled. This was awkward.

"Come across when you're ready. I heard Eileen was bringing donuts."

"See you soon," said Anna. When Lou turned the corner, Anna asked Aunt Lisa, "Do we really need to go? We get it. It's a disease. Mom isn't an asshole; she's a sick asshole."

"Go," said Aunt Lisa.

"It's not fair." Anna groaned. "I feel like my whole life has been about doing whatever because of her." Eli tried not to think that *whatever* referred to her. "I don't want to go to a meeting because *she* has to go to meetings. I don't want to spend more time thinking about it. I want to live my life."

"I get that."

"So, do I still have to go?"

"Absolutely."

Anna groaned again.

"You got the fuzzy end of the lollipop when it came to parenting, and we both know it. Go spend some time in that room so you don't have to spend your life in this one, okay?"

Anna shook her head, but still said, "Come on, Eli. It's about to start."

Lou, Erica, Teddy, and quiet Anthony were all back tonight and seated in the circle already. Eli and Anna took two of the empty seats as Eileen started the meeting.

"Tonight's topic is rigorous honesty." Knowing smiles crept across the faces of most of the kids in the circle. "You're smiling because we know this one is hard, right? Who wants to share on it?"

"I'll take it," said Erica. "I'm Erica."

"Hi Erica." Still weird.

The meeting went on, and on, and on for another forty-five minutes. It still seemed like everyone was speaking a foreign language: rigorous honesty, inventory, co-dependence. Rigorous honesty sounded like a terrible idea. How could these people—who claimed to have the same experiences that she did—think that lying wasn't anything other than an essential survival skill? If Eli and Anna hadn't been excellent liars, they would have been in foster care right now.

After the circle and holding hands, Erica turned to Eli and Anna. "So, bowling?"

Eli surprised herself with her answer, not daring to pause or look at Anna before giving it. "Yeah, we're in."

"Great," Erica said as she turned to gather everyone else.

"You're dead to me," said Anna, squeezing the flesh on Eli's arm.

Eli ignored her. She wouldn't even let herself flinch.

*   *   *

Strike 3 was on the outskirts of Oxbridge.

"This place looks like a freaking horror movie. I can't believe you brought me here," hissed Anna as they climbed out of Erica's car. "Seriously, when we get abducted, it's going to be your fault."

Eli just laughed. "Come on, you might have fun. Really. You might. You want to go home and fight with Aunt Lisa instead? Because I'll tell her that I wanted to try to connect, to make friends, to participate in the *fellowship*. And that you wouldn't let me. And then the two of you can talk about that until dawn. That sound like a better Friday night to you?"

Anna rolled her eyes but followed. They both bristled at the sight of the two leather-jacket-clad men smoking cigarettes by the entrance. They were wearing Harley-Davidson tank tops stretched over their bellies, red bandannas covering what Eli was sure was greasy hair. The smoke seemed to disappear into their frizzy, red beards. Eli and Anna looked down when they walked by the men.

"Hey Anthony, hey Lou," the men said as the group passed through.

"What's up?" said Lou, giving one a high five.

"Happy Friday, Dave," said Anthony as he walked inside. Eli and Anna looked back at them, baffled.

"My dad used to work here," said Lou.

"My mom plays in the league with her sober friends. It's like her new thing instead of the bar. Dave and Mike own the place. They'll hook us up with free shoes."

The inside was not better than the outside. Just as dark and with a smell that could only be described as damp. Eli and Anna handed over their sneakers and put on the clunky red-and-white bowling shoes. Cyndi Lauper blared through the crackling speakers.

"This place is like a time machine," Anna said.

"Just be nice," Eli said.

"Rigorous honesty," Anna said with an elbow to Eli's ribs.

The group set up at the farthest lane, away from the two competing mom groups and some of Dave and Mike's biker friends who were very, very excited about their most recent spare.

"You're up, Anna," said Teddy, who was sitting on a bench by the lane, his arm around Lou.

"I, um, someone else can go."

"We haven't played in a long time," offered Eli.

"Oh yeah? Not a lot of family bowling trips?" Erica smirked. "Don't worry about it. We can literally all relate."

"Yup," said Teddy.

"Yup," said Anthony.

"I mean, I played a lot," said Lou. "And then my dad would stay here and get drunk with his buddies while I fell asleep on this bench right here. Lots of memories in this good old place."

Everyone laughed. It felt good to laugh, even about something so messed up. Maybe especially about something so messed up. It made Eli feel not quite so alone.

"So, I don't get it," said Eli. "If you guys come from families as functional as mine, how can you think that this whole honesty thing is a good idea? Or don't any of you have cops who knock on the door and credit card companies who call up the house?" Eli couldn't help but notice that now these virtual strangers knew more about her life at home than Javi and Meena.

"I get that. I mean, let's be honest, guys . . . let's be honest about the fact that we are all really, really good liars," said Erica.

Everyone laughed again.

"Like, if my GPA was based solely on my lying skills, I would get into Harvard no problem," said Lou.

"If lying was an Olympic sport—" started Teddy, but everyone was laughing again before he could finish.

"Maybe Anthony's not even my real name—you guys would never know."

"Oh! Anthony's got jokes!" Teddy knighted him with a French fry.

"Tell me if you've heard this one," said Lou. " 'Oh, no, he can't come to the phone right now, he's sick,' when my dad was passed out on the couch, or 'I'll just walk home, my dad is having car trouble,' because he forgot to pick me up from school because he went to the bar instead." Lou's dad, who used to get drunk in this bowling alley. Lou's dad, who was dead now. Everyone nodded and was quiet. "Those lies didn't do shit to protect me; they just protected him. All they did was make sure that no one could help me. And in the end, they didn't protect him anyway, because he's dead."

A small bell rang inside Eli. *All they did was make sure that no one could help me.* She heard Javi's voice, hurt and angry. *It's like you're so busy "protecting" me, you don't even give me a chance to be a good friend to you.* She closed her eyes and let the bell ring.

"So, anyway, dead dads are a bummer. How did you two end up here?" asked Lou, pulling Eli back to the bowling alley, and to the strangers she'd lied to less than her own best friends.

"Yeah," added Anthony. "Incredibly nosy minds who wish to change the subject want to know." He nodded in Lou's direction. "It's okay—you don't have to tell us anything."

"But you should," said Teddy, handing a ball to Eli. "Because we are incredibly nosy. You're up, bro." Eli smiled at the word.

"She's not your bro—she's my sister," Anna said.

Eli was annoyed. She didn't need Anna to make Teddy feel weird for calling her "bro" or "little man." She wasn't even sure that she minded it. And if he really thought she was a guy, this was about to get awkward as hell.

"No reason she can't be both, right?" Teddy said.

Eli took the ball.

"Right," she said.

Both. Maybe that was the word for it. She didn't feel like a bro, but she knew what Teddy was trying to say. They were alike, and not just because of their alcoholic moms or their mops of blond hair. Teddy wasn't what he seemed—Mr. America. And Eli wasn't quite what she seemed either—a boy or a girl, depending on who was looking. He wasn't a regular boy, and she wasn't a regular girl, and if his word for that was *bro*, maybe it could be hers too. She squared her shoulders to try on the title. She rolled a spare, for the first time in her life. When she came back to the bench, Anna was midway through the story they'd told so many times already. But this time, it was different. This time, they didn't leave out anything.

* * *

When they'd gotten back to Aunt Lisa's, Champ had woken up from his snoozing spot on the porch and followed them inside. Now, he was snoring at their feet, the cabin creaking even though no one was up.

"I have to tell you something," Eli said.

"Is it that you told me so? Because I know, okay; it was fun. I can admit it. Like, lame, dork fun, but still. Not a bad night."

"It's not that. But thank you. I will take your heartfelt appreciation."

"What is it?"

"The honesty thing. I can't stop thinking about it. I always thought I wasn't hurting anyone by lying to them, or by just not telling them something, like I was just doing my job."

"Yeah, me too. What's your point?"

"My point is that you asked me if I had said anything about Peterson. And literally speaking, like quite literally, I hadn't. But I did *do* something. And I think that means I lied to you."

"I knew it. What did you do?"

Eli took a deep breath. "He came up to me after parent-teacher conferences and said that he hadn't seen Mom at the bar lately—I guess the Spotted Dog is near his house. And he said that he knew it was you at conferences, and that the only way he wouldn't go to the principal about us being on our own was if you came down to see him. And I wasn't going to let that happen. And so I made the signs. I put them in all of his roll books; I put them in the girls' gym bags. I didn't tell anyone about it, about you, and I didn't tell anyone what you told me. I wouldn't do that. But I did have something to do with what happened to him. I didn't tell you because I didn't think I could tell anyone, it felt like such a big deal. I saw Charmaine's lawyer mom going into the school, and I thought I should make sure that no one could trace it back to me, and if they could, that they would never trace it back to you. And I'm sorry that I lied to you, but I'm not sorry I did that." Eli realized she'd kept her eyes closed the entire time she'd been talking. She opened them. There were tears on Anna's face. This week she'd seen Anna cry more than she'd seen her cry in her entire life.

Anna grabbed Eli by the arms and threw her into a hug. She held Eli so close to her that Eli couldn't hear what she was saying.

"What?" Eli asked.

"I said, 'thank you.'"

—23—

WHEN AUNT LISA went back to work on Monday, Eli and Anna had to work on the garden. Living in an apartment, they had never spent this much time outside before. They didn't know begonias from petunias or weeds from stems. So, after Aunt Lisa got home each night, they spent time replanting and repairing the mistakes they'd made that day. Tonight, Aunt Lisa was showing Eli how to properly space the lettuce patch they were supposed to replace the next day. Aunt Lisa was in her "gardening pants" (which, as far as Eli was concerned, were pretty much as dirt-covered and grass-stained as her regular pants) and was showing her the difference between a trowel and a spade. But Eli's hands kept going to her pockets, as if her phone was vibrating. It wasn't.

"Eli, do you work for the CIA? Are you waiting on an important call?"

"Sorry. I miss my friends," Eli said, feeling a boulder appear in her throat out of nowhere.

"Just a few more days now."

"I know. But I'm not sure they'll be happy to see me."

"Huh. Is this that kid, your principal's son? His mom said he was pretty worried about you."

"Pretty pissed at me is more like it."

"Eh, pissed and worried are cousins. Just look at Anna. You can't tell me that she's that pissed at your mom because she's *not* worried about her."

"He's one of my best friends. And when we left, we just left. I didn't tell him anything. I never tell him anything."

"People love you, Eli."

Eli didn't know what love had to do with it. "I don't think he'll ever talk to me again."

"Write him a letter. I've had to do that when I was trying to make things right with someone who didn't trust me anymore because I'd hurt them."

"Like Mom?"

"Sure." She stopped digging up the dirt and patting it down, came onto her knees, and looked to the sky. Eli could tell that she wasn't just talking about Mom. She wondered who else it might be, and if that's why she thought she'd seen a tear in Aunt Lisa's eye during the last verse of "I Will Always Love You."

Aunt Lisa snapped back to attention. "Like with your mom, I never thought it worked, she never answered me, but here you guys are. So, you never know."

That night, while Aunt Lisa was at her meeting and Anna was FaceTiming with Jason, Eli sat on the porch with Champ and tried to write. She'd never written a letter before. It felt so odd to be there with a pencil and paper like it was an assignment for school.

> *Dear Javi,*
> *I'm not sure you want to hear from me right now. I understand that. When you did want to hear from me, I wouldn't let you. Now I'm here, and you're not sure you can trust me.*
> *I have never had two weeks as insane as these two weeks. I've learned a lot. I've learned how to drive (!), and how to survive only off of diner food, how to escape the clutches of social workers (twice),*

and how to really, really screw up friendships that are very important to me. And I've learned a little about telling the truth.

The truth is, my mom is an alcoholic. She has been my whole life. There are good days and bad days, but that's the way it is. I thought you'd never be able to understand, but I know now that I never gave you a chance to. And you showed me over and over that you did understand, that you weren't judging me or her, that you just wanted to be my friend. I was too scared to let you. I'm sorry. I'd never had a friend before you and Meena, and I didn't want to screw it up. And that's exactly how I screwed it up. Funny, I guess. There's probably a word in Latin for that. You probably know it. I miss you.

I'm in Vermont now, with my Aunt Lisa. I'm safe, and I'm doing okay. I'm coming home Saturday. I hope you'll give me another chance. I promise to tell you everything.

Love,

Eli

Aunt Lisa had left an envelope with a stamp on it on the counter. It felt so weird to send Javi a letter, but her texts had gone unanswered and she figured if the worst thing that could happen was that he didn't want to talk to her, well, that was already happening. Worth a try.

She sent a text to Meena.

Hi

Meena responded right away.

hi

How are you?

Okay. Are you ever coming back here?

Saturday

Are you coming back to school?

Yeah, Javi's mom is letting me finish the year.

Cool.

Yeah. Um. I miss you.

I miss you too. Now that I've recovered from the freaking heart attack you gave me.

Sorry about that.

You can make it up to me.

I promise to try.

Eli nearly dropped the phone when she saw the heart-eyes emoji pop up in Meena's reply. She had no idea what it meant. Obviously, it was something good. But was Meena saying that she had feelings for her? That there was hope? No, she wouldn't let herself think that. But heart-eyes, that's got to mean love. It didn't necessarily mean romantic love, though. Screw it, Eli decided.

Three hearts. Unmistakable. Like the three of them.

—24—

AFTER DAYS IN the garden and evenings redoing it, Anna and Eli were tan, dirt-covered, and nearly done. Wednesday afternoon, they chopped the wood to replace the side of the flower bed they'd run over.

"You're like a page out of a Young Homosexuals of America calendar, PB," Anna said as Eli swung the ax.

"Yes, yes, I am." Eli smiled. They nailed the plank in and then set up the sprinklers to run water over the zucchini and the begonias that they had finally planted in the right place. It was kind of a jigsaw puzzle itself, all the right seeds nestled in the right patches of dirt, the neat lines separating lettuce from tomatoes from begonias from bleeding hearts.

Inside the house, Aunt Lisa's landline started to ring. Eli looked at Anna and jutted her head towards the front door. *You're the big sister*, her chin indicated. *You get it.* Anna tossed down the hose and stormed inside.

"Well, this is a first," said Anna as she came back and sat on a patch of grass near the garden.

"What?"

"Aunt Lisa says we need to make dinner for ourselves. She has a date. She literally said, 'Don't wait up.'"

"Go, Aunt Lisa!"

"Do you think we'll get to meet her girlfriend?"

"I bet we already know her. There are like five people in this town."

"It's hard to imagine . . ."

"Aunt Lisa on a date?"

"Yeah, kind of."

"She's probably still wearing that same sweatshirt from yesterday . . ."

"Her Tuesday sweatshirt," they said in unison. It was easy to laugh at Aunt Lisa's style (lumberjack-meets-soldier-meets-yoga-teacher, Anna called it), but still, Eli couldn't help thinking about what it might be like to go on a date like that herself. To sit across from a woman (okay, across from Meena, hopefully) who wanted to be there just as much as she did, not caring what anybody thought. She wondered if they'd hold hands under the table. Have a goodnight kiss. Eli blushed, and shook her head. It was difficult, and kind of creepy, to imagine Aunt Lisa kissing anyone.

Even though Aunt Lisa had said not to wait up, they did. They finished the chores around the farm (as they called the yard when Aunt Lisa wasn't in earshot), feeding and watering the chickens, and setting out food for Champ (who always left the kibble in favor of chasing a stray rodent). Eli also put some carrots out for the rabbits who hopped around near the edge of the trees at sunset. They made dinner—well, they made eggs, toast, and bacon, because when your options are rabbit, venison ("Bambi!" they had both screamed), and a plastic baggie of something red and squishy labeled "Parts," you make breakfast and call it dinner. They washed the dishes, swept the floors, made the sofa into a bed, and generally made excuses to stay up, hoping to catch a glimpse of the mystery woman—or at least of Aunt Lisa's "in love" face.

When she finally came in, Eli and Anna were sitting at the table, trying a gradient jigsaw puzzle and failing to tell the difference between light blue and light light blue. Aunt Lisa came in, closed the door hard, and went to her room without speaking. They turned out the lights, pretended to get ready for bed. Anna went to brush her teeth, and Eli went to spy.

"Jane, thanks for picking up."

It was all kinds of wrong to eavesdrop on someone's conversation with their sponsor, of course, but Eli certainly couldn't help the fact that the cabin was small, the walls were thin, and she was just sitting on her bed (impossibly still so as not to make a sound so that she could hear every word, but whatever).

"I fell for it again. I'm such an idiot. Adam called me, asked me to meet him for a drink . . . no, no, of course I didn't . . . no, coffee. But I went and he just did what he always does, you know, let's get back together, I promise it'll be different this time, but I could smell the booze on his breath . . . Yeah, okay. I will . . . I can't say I'm grateful, but okay . . . I'll try . . . No, I know that's the right thing . . . Yeah, I'm going to sleep. I think I freaked out the girls when I came in . . . Okay. Thank you. Good night."

Eli turned off the lights and texted Anna.

It's not her girlfriend, it's her ex, and his name is Adam.

Anna shot out of the bathroom.

"Shhhh!" whispered Eli.

"Shove over and tell me everything," whispered Anna as she pushed Eli over on the bed.

"I don't know anything," Eli said.

"That's not true, snoop."

"Okay, fine. She seems to have an ex, named Adam, who I think is an alcoholic too, and he wanted to get back together, but she said no, and it sounds like Jane doesn't like him."

"You're sure it was Adam? Not Andrea? Amanda?"

"Adam. He. Trust me when I say I'm more surprised than you are."

"I'm sorry that you're down a gay role model."

Eli elbowed Anna in the ribs. "You know what's harder to imagine than Aunt Lisa's girlfriend?"

"Aunt Lisa's boyfriend," they said together, stifling each other's giggles.

"Was she sad?" Anna asked.

"Yeah, I think she was crying." They both got quiet. It was less funny to think of Aunt Lisa, who could skin a deer from head to hoof without a twinge of remorse, brought to tears by some guy, some Adam. Above the cabin, the sky opened suddenly, loud drops pouring down, pelting the wood roof, pelting the newly planted garden, pelting Champ, who slept, unbothered, on the porch.

Aunt Lisa woke them up as usual the next morning, like nothing was wrong. She was in her usual Thursday sweatshirt; she was just as grumpy and demanding as she always was before her coffee. "Guys. Eggs. Now."

Instead of putting up a fight (even though she never won, she always fought), this time Anna just rolled over, threw on her jeans, and nudged Eli out of bed. They went out back to face down the chicken coop yet again.

"Only a few more rounds of Eli versus Attila the Hen to go. You got this."

"Oh, my dear sister, thank you for your support," snarked Eli as she stuck her hand in the coop to reach for eggs. She passed the eggs to Anna, who carried a basket now after learning her lesson the first time.

"We only have a few days left here. I can't believe I'm going to say this but," Anna said, looking up at the sky, down at her wet feet in the grass. The sound of the owls reminded them that it was still really, really early. "I've kind of gotten used to this."

"Me too." Silently, they made their way to the front of the house. Aunt Lisa was sitting in her usual chair, but she wasn't meditating like she did every morning. She was just sitting, head in her hands, staring at nothing. She sniffed when Eli and Anna came around the corner, and sat up straight.

"Thanks guys. This is good," she said, reaching for the basket without looking at them.

"Are you okay?" asked Anna.

"Yeah, sorry," said Aunt Lisa, shaking her head like she was trying to shake the tears that were welling up in her eyes back down.

"Is it Adam?" Eli asked.

"You really are a Grade A snoop, kid," said Aunt Lisa.

"The walls are thin."

"Go inside. Those eggs aren't going to cook themselves."

When they sat down at the table, passing the plate of eggs around, pouring coffee, and adding milk, Eli and Anna stayed quiet.

Aunt Lisa took a deep breath. "Yes, it's Adam, okay?"

"Is he your ex?" asked Anna, taking on a woman-to-woman, I've-got-a-past-too tone that annoyed Eli.

"Yes. And he wants to get back together, but it's not a good idea. So, I'm sad. That's what you saw on the porch; that's what you saw last night. That's all."

"Why don't you want to get back together?"

"He's a drunk."

"So? So are you."

"Yeah, but he's not sober. I stayed with him for my first three years, hoping that he'd follow my example. But he didn't. Until he is, unless he is, we can't be together."

"Why would you want to be with someone who's that much of a mess?"

"Well, first of all, when we first got together, I was a mess too. Second of all, I'm six feet tall, I hunt, I can lift two hundred pounds easy, I don't wear makeup. Most guys . . ." She trailed off.

"Most guys think you're gay," said Eli, boldly.

"Yup. Most nieces do too," Aunt Lisa said, smiling for the first time that morning. "But I'm not, and it can be hard to find the right guy who gets me."

"No offense," Anna said. "But it sounds like this Adam guy doesn't get you. Or at least, he doesn't get the new you. You deserve to be with someone who works as hard as you do to not be a mess."

"That's the nicest thing you've ever said to me, Anna."

"It's the nicest thing she's ever said to anyone."

Anna kicked Eli under the table. "For real, though—you talk all this shit about how I should value myself and go to college and take myself seriously. I'm not trying to be mean, but maybe you should take your own advice?"

"I probably should," Aunt Lisa said, staring far out the window before shaking her head again. "Okay, I'm going to work. Do not burn the house down," she said, the same way she did every day, and then walked out the door without another word.

With the garden done, there wasn't much left to do but homework. And by 11:07 A.M., Eli was not in the mood for it. The sun was shining, there was a warm breeze through the window, and here they were in a pretty place (well, it seemed pretty to them now) stuck inside with worksheets.

"Are you busy?" Eli asked.

Anna looked at her out of the corner of her eye. "If you call staring at the same three sentences about the glory of trigonometry over and over busy, then yes I am. Industrious, even."

"I can't think either."

"You nervous about Saturday?" Two more days until they had to go get Mom.

"I guess. I just don't want to get my hopes up."

"Yeah. Same."

"Are you going to see the Jacket when we get back?"

"Yeah. Are you going to see Meeeeeeena?"

"I hope so. We've been texting."

"Oooooooh," Anna said, and flicked a pencil at her sister's head. "Okay, screw this. Let's go."

"Where are we going?"

"We're just going."

"But Aunt Lisa—"

"Is working. She won't miss us. We'll be back by the end of the day. But you know as well as I do that we're not going to last another minute in here."

When they went outside, the warm air hit them in the face, making them laugh, blind from the sun.

"Let's go for a walk."

"To where? We're in the middle of nowhere."

"To somewhere."

They set out down the hill, onto the main road. They were still far from town when Eli spotted the couple she'd seen on campus her first day there. They were both wearing black sports bras and board shorts, with towels over their shoulders and flip-flops on their feet.

"This way," she said to Anna.

"You just want to play follow-the-homosexuals."

"Will you just trust a snoop for a second? I'm right about this," Eli said, though she knew that Anna was right too. As they walked, they saw a girl in a sundress, towel over her shoulder. Some laughing boys approached from the opposite direction with wet hair and no shirts.

"Okay, okay, I'm with you now," Anna said.

Eli rolled her eyes, smiling. The trail wound down a steep hill and across a wide field of wildflowers with some cows grazing in the distance. They were making their way through the trees on the edge of the field, and Anna was complaining about ticks and cow patties, when they saw it. The river ran wide, deep, and loud, blue through the brown and green of the trees. There were shouts and laughter, a girl jumping in from a tire swing someone had rigged onto an old tree by the riverbank. Couples lay out on blankets in the sun-filled clearing, the tall grass rolling like waves in the warm breeze.

Anna and Eli exchanged barely a glance before hanging their shirts on the nearest tree. Anna jumped in first, doing a flip off the tire swing as she landed. Eli followed closely behind with a splash. She dunked her head back, feeling the water rush into her ears, drowning out the happy shouts of all the other bathers.

They floated downstream together, Eli's hands around Anna's feet, Anna guiding them away from the shore. Eli watched the sun through the trees, the yellow-green-white spots it made on her belly, her legs, the water. With her arms stretched overhead, she could feel all her muscles individually using their power to grip on to Anna. It didn't hurt; it felt good, powerful. Her legs felt strong as they kicked past the rocks that threatened to get in the way. She even liked her belly, the way it kept her floating, the way it moved in and out with her breath. She inhaled the smell of the green, the sun, the water and watched her belly rise and fall. Water always reminded her that she was just an animal. A human animal, but still. Everyone seemed so hung up on categories—male, female, gay, straight, boy, girl— but really, animal seemed like the only category that applied to everyone. In her animal body, she felt right at home. Girl and boy are just lies to make us forget where we come from, Eli thought.

Anna kicked her feet, and Eli let go. They rested on twin rocks poking through the water by the river's edge.

"You know you have to leave, right?" Eli broke their happy silence.

"We both do, duh."

"No, I mean you. How many days until graduation? I know you're keeping count."

"Oh my god with the relentless snooping already!"

"Seriously, though. What are you going to do?"

"I don't know, PB. Look at the craziness of the last few months. How can I think about the future?"

"Because you have to. You think that just because you're kind of a jerk most of the time that I don't know that the reason you won't even let yourself say the word *college* is because of me. You've given me enough of your life, Banana. I'll be okay. But if you give up any more of yourself to save me, I don't know what you'll have left. Maybe just the anger."

Anna looked up, squinting at the sun, and dunked her ponytail in the cool water. "You'd be lost without me," Anna said with a smile.

"Yeah," Eli said. "But you'll be lost if you stay. Just think about it, okay?"

"Sure."

"For real," Eli said, looking her sister right in the eye. "You did a good job with me. It's your turn now."

"And if I fail? Like everyone else in our damn family?"

"And if you never try? What kind of example would that set for your iddy-biddy baby sister?" Eli made a baby face to match her baby voice.

Anna laughed, and Eli splashed her. Anna splashed back. A water war later they were happy, laughed-out, tired. They walked slowly all the way back to Aunt Lisa's.

That night, Teddy called to say that everyone was getting together for a bonfire at the river, and did she and Anna want to come.

"Hard pass," said Anna, who had been talking nonstop for the last three hours about her upcoming FaceTime date with Jason.

"Yeah, okay, I'll come," said Eli. She hung up and turned to Aunt Lisa. "Okay?"

Aunt Lisa nodded, not looking up from the dinner she was cooking, but Eli could tell she was smiling.

"Be back by ten. Tomorrow's your last day. You'll have to pack, and I don't want you dragging your butt all over because you didn't get your beauty rest, okay?"

"Yup, thanks!"

Teddy's truck came up the drive, and Eli felt silly and cool at the same time as she pulled herself up into the cab.

"Thanks for coming, bud," he said. "Are you going to miss us? The wild times in Oxbridge?"

Eli laughed. "Kinda, yeah. I don't know. It's been kind of like a vacation from my life, you know?

"That sounds pretty sweet," he said. "I could use one of those."

After a moment, Eli asked him suddenly, "Why are you so nice to me?"

"What do you mean?"

"I mean, blond dudes with trucks who play sports and like girls don't tend to be nice to me. They tend to push me into lockers."

"They sound like assholes. I'm not an asshole."

"That simple, huh?"

"Yeah, also, I don't know. You remind me of me. Bet that doesn't make any sense."

"No," said Eli. "You remind me of me, too."

They rolled down their windows, arms stretched out like planes through the air.

The bonfire was the closest thing to a party that Eli had ever been to. The clearing by the river looked different than it had earlier that afternoon. The stars were out, the banks of the river turned orange and black by the flames and the shadows. Lou, Erica, and Anthony were sitting on a log in front of the fire. Other kids that she'd seen at meetings before were there too, everyone spread out enjoying the fire and the darkness. Teddy hopped out of the truck, grabbing blankets and a guitar from the bed.

"Oh, get ready for a proper Teddy sing-along!" shouted Lou when she saw him.

"You have to let me warm up first," Teddy said over Lou's laugh.

"Give me those chips," he demanded.

There was a cooler next to where the group was sitting. Eli approached it, curiously.

"It's all soda, little dude," Teddy said behind her. "I don't know about you but alcohol . . ."

"Scares the crap out of you?"

"Pretty much. Maybe it won't always, but for now, I'd rather stick with the demons I already have."

"Exactly. Like, how many times can they tell us we're basically bound to become drunks the second we pick up a drink?"

"It's hereditary, you know," they said in unison and laughed.

"You know what I'm going to miss most about you freaks?" Eli asked.

"What's that?"

"Literally no one else thinks alcoholism is funny."

Teddy punched her in the shoulder. She would miss that too. The way that Teddy treated her like one of the boys without ever asking, without making it a big deal. She had always loved being Anna's little sister, even when it was hard, but it was pretty nice being Teddy's little brother too.

"Teddy, you and your mini-me need to get your butts over here," Lou yelled.

They sat on a blanket by the fire and Teddy started to play. In between the songs and the snacks, they fell into stories. Anthony said that when he was little his dad used to have all of his buddies over until late at night, to show Anthony off, making him tap dance for them (Anthony? Tap dancing?), and how much he hated it. He quit dancing, became quite shy, and had a hard time making friends, but he felt like that had been getting better recently. He glanced up and smiled.

"Awww, we love you, Anthony," said Erica and Lou, and they forced him into an enormous hug.

Eli told them about Javi, about Meena, about how even though these two weeks had been weird as hell, it had been nice not to think about Kevin waiting for her, planning his revenge.

"You should punch him again, just the first thing as soon as you get back to school. Show him you haven't lost your touch," said Lou.

"That's pretty much the worst advice I've ever heard," said Erica.

"Teach him to mess with you," Lou muttered, cracking her knuckles.

"This one goes out to you, little dude," Teddy said, lowering his voice and adopting a southern drawl. "It's called 'A Boy Named Sue,' by Mr. Johnny Cash." Keeping the ridiculously low voice and the accent, Teddy sang a silly song about a boy who wanted to kill his father for giving him the name Sue, and how he ended up being proud of who he was, how it made him stronger. "My name is Sue! How do you doooooo!!!" Teddy howled into the night sky.

"Maybe if Kevin's dad had named him Sue instead, he wouldn't be such a dick," Teddy said when the song was done, reaching for the chips.

It started feeling late, but Eli kicked tiredness from her mind. She wanted this night to stretch to morning, straight through Friday, into next year. They played kickball in the dark until Erica and Michelle's phones started ringing like crazy.

"Michelle, we gotta go. Shit, it's later than I thought."

"What time is it?" asked Eli, patting her jeans for her phone, then seeing it clearly in her mind on the bookshelf by the front door.

"It's one."

"A.M.?" Eli knew the answer, of course; she was just desperately hoping that by some miracle Erica meant eleven, or maybe even the very civilized nine-thirty. Not, technically speaking, an hour into the following day.

"I'll take you home, kid." As Teddy drove, Eli could practically hear Aunt Lisa pacing and Anna yelling at her.

When they pulled into Longmeadow Lane, Eli said, "Teddy, I want to have this long, meaningful goodbye with you, but with every passing second my aunt and my sister are closer to murdering me, so I have to go.

Thank you for everything, bro," she said, and punched him in the arm as she hopped out of the truck. He honked once as she stepped onto the porch, and his headlights backed down the drive, disappearing into the darkness. She wished she could do the same instead of opening the door. It swung open.

"Oh thank freaking god," said Anna. She didn't say anything else, didn't yell in her usual Anna way; there was no tirade about where the hell were you, what were you thinking, do you know what time it is. She just walked to the farthest end of the cabin and looked out the window so that she didn't have to look at Eli.

"Okay, then," said Aunt Lisa, getting up from the couch where she had been sitting, her hands clasped together, head down. "Are you drunk?"

"What? No! I was with a bunch of kids from freaking Alateen. You know, the place you make us go to deal with all the terrible crap that alcohol has done to our lives without us even drinking it? No, I am not drunk."

"Just inconsiderate then. Good night." Aunt Lisa went into her room and closed the door. When everything is silent, and your aunt and your sister are so angry with you they can't speak, a door closing sounds like a slam.

"You're mad too, Anna? Really? Do you not remember my scooping you up off the bathroom floor like a month ago? Do you not remember how you didn't come home for *days* so you could live in la-la land with Jason?"

Anna just stared out the window for what felt like forever. Finally she said, "I thought you were dead." She crossed the room, pushed past Eli, and went outside. She closed the door, and Eli heard another slam. She looked out the window and saw Anna sit down on the chair on the porch, wrapping herself in a blanket.

Eli threw on pajamas and turned the couch into a bed for the second-to-last time. She would sit here and wait for Anna to come to her senses and come inside. Anna, who had scared her so many times too. Eli had lost track of time, and had forgotten her phone—that was pretty different from being blackout drunk on the bathroom floor of a bar. She crossed her arms. She was sorry, of course, that she'd scared them. But when she dipped her head down and smelled the woodsmoke still on her clothes, when she breathed in and could still taste the night air, could hear the sound of belly laughter for funny stories and awful ones, she wasn't sure she wouldn't do it all again.

* * *

"Get up. Get eggs." Aunt Lisa stood over Eli, who didn't remember falling asleep. All the lights were still on; Anna had never come to bed. "Get your sister."

Eli's body hurt. The smell of smoke on her clothes, her hair, her skin had left her mouth sand-dry. She swallowed hard. Anna had fallen asleep in the rocking chair. Sometimes—usually when she wasn't speaking, or better yet, wasn't awake—Eli could see all the Annas. Not just goth, angry Anna, but soccer Anna, or Anna who had dance parties in the kitchen with Mom. Right now, with her lashes against what used to be big baby cheeks, her skinny body wrapped in a blanket for warmth, Eli could see seven-year-old Anna, pulling the covers around both of them as she tried to get three-year-old Eli to "camp" with her in the fort she'd made in the living room.

"Anna, eggs," Eli said, shaking her awake.

"You get them," Anna said, stretching, shivering slightly and going inside. Close. Slam.

The yard was wet with dew, and Eli's shoes were soaked by the time she got to the blue chicken coop.

"Hey, beautiful," she said as she reached her hand in. "I'll be quick, thank you so much for the amazing eggs." Her voice sounded flat, hollow. Attila pecked her hand eight times before she had taken more than six eggs—half her usual haul. On the ninth time, the hen drew blood. Eli dropped the basket, and three of the eggs cracked.

"Damn it," she shouted, and kicked the basket, breaking the rest. The yard was beautiful this time of day, the sun rising over the hill and making warm spots in the wet grass, birdsong ringing out from every tree, blue sky bursting through every green leaf. And here was Eli, bleeding, cursing, yolk sticking to her wet shoes, her face red, her throat tight.

"Let's go, kid," said Aunt Lisa, putting one rough hand on Eli's shoulder. She guided her through the house, into the bathroom. "Sit."

She held Eli's hand and grabbed some cotton swabs. She cleaned the scratches out, and Eli tried not to wince. She was embarrassed to have Aunt Lisa cleaning her up, like she was a little kid with a boo-boo.

"There," Aunt Lisa said, putting ointment and a Band-Aid on Eli's hand. "Just keep it dry." At least she didn't offer to kiss it and make it better.

"I'm sorry about breakfast," Eli said, looking down.

"The problem isn't breakfast," Aunt Lisa said, leaving the bathroom. Eli stormed after her, fed up, embarrassed, still wearing yolk-covered shoes.

"Then what's the problem? I had a little fun? I stayed out too late, sure, and I'm sorry about that, but since when is that the worst thing that anyone in this family has done? Am I just here to clean up messes? Don't I get to make my own?"

Aunt Lisa and Anna were sitting at the table. The blanket was still around Anna's shoulders, and she was sipping a cup of coffee. Both of them looked at her like she was an alien.

"You want to answer that, Anna?" Aunt Lisa asked.

"Not really," said Anna.

Aunt Lisa cleared her throat.

"Okay, fine. The problem is you're an idiot if you think I'm mad because you had a good time."

"Try again," said Aunt Lisa, low but not angry.

Anna sighed. "Eli, the problem is that you scared me. You scared us both. You left your phone, we didn't know where you were or if you were okay, and we had no way of finding out. And then you think we're mad that you had a good time. Idiot. I'm mad because you're my entire world, Eli, the whole entire thing. And you can't even see it." It was silent except for the birds singing like nothing was wrong.

"Why don't you sit down, Eli," said Aunt Lisa in a way that was definitely not a question. Eli sat without speaking, without thinking, and finally looked up at her sister. Anna's face had black stains from her eyes to her chin, rivers of mascara not only from today's tears, but from last night too, tracks of worry down her face.

"I'm sorry," said Eli softly.

"I don't care," said Anna.

"Try again," said Aunt Lisa.

"I know you're sorry. But you don't need to be. You're allowed to have a good time, of course you are. And you're allowed to mess up," she softened, suddenly, tears turning the black streaks back into rivers. Anna's anger was like a tornado, it tore through—taking off roofs, lifting cows sheer off the ground, turning over cars—but then it was gone just as soon as it came. Especially when she was angry at Eli. Eli's head was hanging down to her chest, but when she glanced up at Anna, she could see that the anger was gone, the fear was starting to go too. "I just want you to hear me. You matter to me. I know I can be selfish, but you can forget that your self matters to any of us at all. I just want you to treat yourself like you matter. Because you matter so much to me."

"Okay."

"I love you, PB. You freaking idiot." She pulled Eli's chair to her and hugged her until Eli was gasping.

"Too . . . tight!"

"I! LOVE! YOU! DO! YOU! UNDERSTAND!"

Anna was laughing now, as she hugged her so tight that

Eli ended up on her lap, hugged her from side to side until they both fell onto the floor.

Aunt Lisa laughed her barky laugh and said, "All right, good. Now get up off my floor."

"Admit it," Anna said, grinning at Aunt Lisa from the floor. "We're a whole lot more exciting than a jigsaw puzzle. You're going to miss us."

"Could be," Aunt Lisa said with a half smile. "Now be quiet so I can meditate." Aunt Lisa walked outside, sat down in her chair, and closed her eyes, smiling fully now.

That night, Aunt Lisa lit a fire in the pit in the backyard.

"Apparently Eli's really into bonfires, so . . ."

"Too soon," said Anna, and they all laughed.

"Are we going to make s'mores?" asked Eli.

"Are we freaking Girl Scouts?" said Anna, rolling her eyes.

"First of all, I would be an excellent Girl Scout," said Aunt Lisa, making them both laugh. "And yeah, sure, go get some sticks. Let's do this thing."

They sat on a blanket near the fire, sticks in hand, marshmallows, graham crackers, and chocolate spread out before them like an offering.

"Give me one," Anna said, nudging Eli in the ribs. Anna roasted her marshmallow slowly, getting it perfectly brown on all sides. Eli stuck hers straight into the flames, watching it catch fire like a tiny explosion at the end of her stick. She liked the way the burnt black flecks stuck to her teeth. Anna, meanwhile, watched as the perfectly browned fluff melted the chocolate just right, not dribbling down her hands, giving no crunch as she bit down.

Aunt Lisa took a deep breath. "So, pick up at Green Hills is at noon. That means we need to leave here by six. That means you need to be up and packed before then."

"None of this sleeping in like we usually do, huh?" Anna was joking, but Aunt Lisa meant business.

"Exactly. Anna, we'll drive your car. I'll fly home on Monday."

They nodded. No one said anything for a few minutes.

In a voice softer than one they'd ever heard her use, Aunt Lisa said, "You guys okay?"

They nodded again. Anna was looking up at the stars. Eli's stomach was losing interest in the s'mores, clutching with nerves now.

"I'm scared everything will be different," Eli said.

"I'm scared everything will be the same," Anna said. They laughed quickly, still nervous.

Anna looked at Eli. "You don't want things to be different? Because our lives were so awesome before this?"

"I mean different like Javi and Meena won't talk to me, I won't have anything to do all summer because they won't want anything to do with me anymore, and I'll start high school getting shoved into the boy's bathroom every time I try to walk down the hall because I'll be all alone again. Okay, I guess that part's the same." Eli looked at Anna as she shifted closer to her on the blanket. "What do you mean you're scared it'll be the same? We'll be together; that's the same."

"Yeah, and I wouldn't change that." Anna dropped her head for a moment to Eli's shoulder. "But I mean that we'll get back, she'll stay sober for three and a half seconds, and then something will happen—the car will need gas or she'll stub her toe or whatever—and we'll back where we started, except that I'll be a senior. And you know, I hear senior year is kind of important, if, you know, I want to go to college." She head-butted Eli's shoulder as she sat up.

"I don't think she's going to relapse," said Eli.

"She might," said Aunt Lisa. "You both need to be prepared for that."

"Thanks, Aunt Sunshine," said Anna.

"Smartass. I was going to say, but you also need to be prepared to be okay no matter what she does. Your mom doesn't get to decide the rest of your lives. If she wants to mess up a life, let it be hers, not yours."

"How can you say that though?" said Eli, angrier than she meant to be. "The waiting up, the worrying, the trying to cover with the landlord, the cops."

"It's not exactly conducive to studying," added Anna. "You don't know what she's like."

"The hell I don't." Both girls looked at her. Aunt Lisa sighed. "Your mom was fearless when we were kids. Fearless, smart, pissed as hell. A lot like you, Anna. I remember being on the school bus, and some kid made fun of me, and she went right up to him and punched him square in the stomach. She got me dressed every morning when our mom was too hungover to get out of bed. She made sure I did my homework and knew how to make dinner appear out of nothing more than cornflakes and ketchup. And our mom, when she was home, spent all of her time tearing Carrie down to make herself feel better. To make her feel like she couldn't make it on her own. You can say what you want about Carrie, Anna, and there's plenty to say, but she's not like that. The only person trying to keep you stuck in Middletown is you."

Eli put her arm around Anna. Nobody spoke for a long time, as the fire sparked and hissed, occasionally rousing Champ from his comfortable post on the blanket between Aunt Lisa and Anna.

"I don't understand why everyone is so sure I can do this," said Anna, finally.

"Because we've watched you do everything else," said Eli.

—25—

THE EVICTION NOTICE wasn't exactly unexpected, but it wasn't the homecoming any of them envisioned, Mom in her institutional sweatpants, Eli, Anna, and Aunt Lisa standing in silence behind her.

"I've got it, Carrie," Aunt Lisa said quietly. And Mom just nodded because what was there to say. Eli and Anna both noticed that this time Mom didn't have any of her usual excuses at the ready, she didn't promise Aunt Lisa she'd pay her back the next day or that she had the money coming in, really, she did. She just nodded, and her shoulders lowered a little.

"Thank you," she said quietly.

Mom called the landlord, and Aunt Lisa gave him two months' back rent and rent for the next three months too. Mom's eyes went wide and she looked like she would cry. Aunt Lisa put her hand on Mom's shoulder. There was pizza for dinner. It was quiet and awkward and a little sad, kind of the same and kind of different, just like Eli and Anna thought. After dinner, they all squished awkwardly onto the couch to watch *The Walking Dead*.

"It's a television show," Anna teased Aunt Lisa, "You know, the box with the bunny ears?"

"Ha ha ha, I thought it was about you in the mornings," Aunt Lisa shot back. Eli saw Mom smiling but she worried that she was jealous of the ease there was between them, the ways that Aunt Lisa, Eli, and Anna had become a unit and that the piece of the puzzle that didn't fit was Mom. It made Eli nervous, a familiar pit in her stomach that hadn't been there for a few months opening up wide, is this it? Would laughter between Aunt Lisa and Anna carry her all the way back to the bar? Eli's nails pressed into her palms. She stared at the TV, even though it wasn't on yet.

During the first commercial, after no fewer than eight zombie attacks that Eli barely registered, Mom turned to Aunt Lisa. Eli cautiously removed her eyes from the floor by the TV and let them travel to Mom's face. She expected to see her lips drawn tight, her hands clenched into fists (Eli got the habit from somewhere, after all), she expected to see the usual traces of pain or anger etched on her mother's face, but instead she saw relief.

"Lisa, I swear, I have no idea where we would be tonight without you. To see you making my kids laugh, to know that they spent the last weeks complaining about early mornings instead of in a foster home, to know that if not for you I would have lost . . ." Mom's voice cracked.

"Please don't tell them this, they'd never let me live it down," Aunt Lisa said, pretending to put her hands over their ears, "but it was good for me too. And I missed you, you know, this was like getting to spend time with the best parts of both of us." Aunt Lisa squeezed her hand. And with that, a zombie roar filled the room again and Anna ordered everyone to cut the mush and pay attention.

The next day, Eli biked over to Javi's house and stood on the doorstep without ringing the bell for what felt like hours. It was probably minutes, maybe even seconds. Finally, she pressed. And waited. More hours, or minutes, or seconds passed. And there he was, wearing his "Omnibus Umbra" t-shirt that she and Meena had gotten him for his birthday last year, not smiling, but not slamming the door, either.

"Hi," she said.

"I got your letter." She blushed and looked down. "I miss you too." She smiled.

He pulled her into an enormous hug. "Don't be dumb again, okay?"

"Okay."

They wandered through his immaculate living room to his room where they sat at either end of his blue couch and just *talked*. They talked about her mom, how it was having her home ("weird, mostly, but I say that a lot lately"), and how she and Anna had convinced the old lady to let them stay at the motel, she told him about Aunt Lisa and Teddy ("he's a total dude bro, but also, totally not") and that she was the one who turned Peterson in. He asked if he could come to her house sometime. She paused for a minute and then said yes.

"You know, it's not like this, it's not like your house."

"Yeah, Eli, I'm not with you for your money, okay?" They both laughed. He told her about how Kevin had been suspended too for a third time that year, and that he heard he was going to a different high school next year. He told her about how King Douchebag seemed like he might be breaking up with his mom, and how he was happy, but also couldn't help feeling like he'd caused it.

"I know I shouldn't complain to you," he said. "After everything you've been through, my problems must seem ridiculous."

"The only ridiculous thing you've said is that," Eli said, giving him a shove. "Problems are problems, I know that your big house doesn't mean everything's perfect."

"I guess."

"Still, though, it must be nice to eat gold-covered bonbons off of gold-covered plates all day. That's what you do, right?"

"Ha! You bet. Are you going to see Meena? I'm late for my afternoon bonbon tasting."

"I want to. I don't know. Everything just feels so . . ."

"Weird?"

She laughed. "Exactly."

"Go see her, weirdo. She's only texted me like 85 times since you got back to see if I've seen you and if you're coming to see her." Eli took that in as Javi shoved her out the door.

She walked the eight minutes from his house to Meena's. Well, to Meena's driveway. She was too scared to go inside. To see her dad.

Meet me by your mailbox.

The door opened and Meena walked down the driveway towards Eli. Eli could feel her heart beating. She could feel the air in her lungs, each individual eyelash as she blinked. She felt her brain send a message to her mouth, *speak*.

"Hi." that was the best she could do.

"Hi, stranger." They walked down to the lake at the end of Meena's road, sitting on the shore with just their toes in the water.

"I was worried you would hate me," Eli said, "worried you already did."

"Why would I hate you?"

"Because of what happened."

"I was worried, Eli, I wasn't angry."

"I meant before that."

"Because I kissed you?"

"I kissed you. And then you threw me off of you. Like it was the grossest thing you'd ever done."

"I was freaked out because of my dad. Not because of you. Not because *I* kissed *you*." And she kissed Eli again.

They looked at each other, smiling. Eli raised her eyebrows.

"You're surprised?"

"I'm happy, and yeah, surprised too." Eli's face felt hot, the corners of her mouth hurt slightly from smiling so hard.

"Surprise," said Meena, and kissed her again. They spent the rest of the afternoon like that, talking and kissing, laughing at the ducks shaking water loose from their feathers, laughing at nothing at all. Eli dug her toes further into the sand, her heart beat its steady rhythm (not the panicked one it was so fond of). Eli closed her eyes and tilted her head back, the sun setting behind her closed lids turning her face a low orange-red.

When she opened her eyes, Meena was still there, resting her head on Eli's shoulder. Eli breathed in the smell of cedar and sunshine in Meena's hair, the weight of her body against her, the warm air and the rustling grass. She closed her eyes again, just for the sheer pleasure of knowing that it would all be there when she opened them.

ONE YEAR LATER

ANNA WAS TAKING forever in the shower.

"Banana, come on!"

"I'm coming, dude, relax." The water stopped. Anna poked her head into Eli's room, hair wrapped in a towel. "I'm not going to be late to my own graduation, fool."

"Jason's going to be here in five minutes."

"I don't care what state of undress he finds me in," Anna said with a cartoonish wink.

"Ew."

Mom came down the hall. "Anna, you're going to be late. We need to have dinner and get out of here."

"The two of you, jeez!"

"You're going to miss us when you're late to absolutely everything next year," Mom said.

"Okay, fine. I'm going. Can everyone relax? I'm the one who's graduating."

"I'm relaxed," said Eli.

"Cool as a cucumber," said Mom. Anna rolled her eyes and went to get dressed.

"Eli, dinner is almost ready. Can you set the table in a few?"

"Sure."

Eli stared out her window a little while longer, thinking about the summer ahead. How different it was from the summer behind. On Monday she was starting her job at the library. It paid minimum wage, but it was free air conditioning and no late fees. Javi was heading off to a classics summer camp in Rome; they were getting together the next day to say goodbye, even Meena was going to come. It was crazy to think that this time last year she was so convinced he was never going to speak to her again.

That felt like a million years ago now, even though Eli could still feel the warm spread of happiness in her stomach when she thought about Meena. Three months after their first kiss, one week after their last one, Meena got the call she'd be waiting for since sixth grade. Not only had she landed a spot on the Robotics Team, the coach invited her to attend Innovative Technology

Charter. ITC was three towns away and had its own electrical engineering lab; each student got to run their own, fully-funded experiments each year. Most students graduated with at least one patent to their name. She called Eli as soon as she hung up with Ms. Sorenson. Eli could hear Meena's voice trembling as she calculated the hours she would be spending getting to school and the hours she would be in the lab and the hours she wouldn't be seeing Eli and Javi. "You have to say yes," Eli told her. "I already did," said Meena, and they both cried. "You better name your first robot after me," Eli said. She could hear Meena smile through the phone. They still saw each other, on the rare weekend that the Robotics Team wasn't competing for their seventh consecutive national title. It wasn't the same, there were no more long kisses by the water, or family game nights, but when Javi, Eli, and Meena got together, they still laughed until their sides hurt, no matter how long it had been.

Javi still met Eli at the door to school every morning, and they walked the halls together, missing the third leg of their triangle. Middletown High had a GSA—just a few kids on a Friday afternoon, but they had the best snacks of any of the clubs. Javi had an enormous crush on Damon, the senior who ran it, and tonight's graduation was going to tear his heart into two. Eli knew how that felt. But she had been distracted lately by Casey, the junior who was going to take over for Damon next year. She was super into film, always trying to make "movie night" a thing, and relating every single conversation to something she'd seen in a movie—usually a gay one. The day the cafeteria served peaches, she couldn't stop talking about *Call Me by Your Name*. Once Javi suggested that reading was fundamental, and they were in for a fifteen-minute lecture about *Paris Is Burning*. It was annoying, maybe. But also kind of cute. It was Eli's summer goal to ask Casey to a movie by the end of August.

"Now, Eli!"

Eli walked into the kitchen to set the table. In some ways, she thought, both her and Anna's fears had come true. Everything was different; everything was the same. Mom had stayed sober, and that was different. She was home, for one thing. And she had a job that she went to every morning no matter what. But like Anthony and Erica and Teddy and Lou had all said, sobriety didn't make any of it perfect. It took getting used to; they were so accustomed to doing everything for themselves.

At first, they were mad at her for being suddenly able to make coffee, cook breakfast, come home at the end of the day—where was that when they'd needed it?

Now they were in high school and perfectly capable of making breakfast, and yes, coffee, and being home alone. There were long fights and slammed doors, and misunderstandings, and a weekend when Anna went to Jason's and told Eli not to tell Mom where she was. But there was also Christmas, like an actual, tree-with-lights-and-presents Christmas where no one got drunk, and no one yelled, and they watched stupid movies until their stomachs ached with laughter.

Other things were the same—money was still tight (Sam's savings account had enough money in it to pay for Anna's books for the next four years, and Mom insisted that they save Eli's for the same thing). Jason and Anna still spent every waking second together. Eli and Anna were still Eli and Anna, and they still worried and fought and kept (just a few) secrets.

"Anna, come on, let's eat!" cried Mom as she pulled the lasagna from the oven. Sobriety hadn't turned Mom into a great cook, but put enough cheese and tomato on anything and it'll taste good.

Jason and Anna emerged from her room. "Hi, Jason," Mom said. "Didn't hear you come in."

"Hi, Ms. Reynolds," he said with an embarrassed smile as he slid into the seat next to Anna's.

"When's Javi coming?" Mom asked.

"He should be here soon."

"You look beautiful, Anna," Mom said. "Don't get anything on your dress before we go!"

"Yep, Mom, I know how to eat," Anna said. They'd had this kind of fight a million times. By now, it just made them both laugh.

"Eli!" Javi shouted from the door. Eli let him in, and he took his seat next to her. A year ago, he had never been to her house. These days, he was over almost as much as Jason.

"Congratulations, Anna," he said as he served himself some lasagna.

"Thanks, Javi. Sorry to disappoint you, but Damon isn't joining us for dinner." Damon was in Anna's AP Psychology course and had been spending lots of time studying at the house with Anna before finals.

"No, no, I'm here with the purest of hearts. Just to celebrate you." He raised a glass.

"Hear, hear," Mom said. "Cheers!"

They clinked glasses and dug in.

"It's good, Ms. Reynolds," said Jason.

"You are a very sweet suck-up, Jason. You are welcome here anytime."

"Or, you know, all the time, apparently," Eli said. Anna kicked her under the table. "Are you guys going to live in the same dorm room next year?"

"Hardy-har-har, nosy. No. University of Massachusetts splits up folks from the same high school."

"Is John coming?" Mom asked. Anna had seen her father a few times in the past year.

"He said so," said Anna. "Is that okay?"

"If he said he'll be there, he'll be there. And of course it is okay."

It was hard to imagine that Mom didn't feel a little sad about John, his beautiful wife, his two well-behaved, sweet kids. Like he was the walking definition of the road not taken. But she never said. She encouraged Anna to stay in touch with him; he'd even written her a letter of recommendation for her college application.

"Is Aunt Lisa meeting us there?"

"Yup, so eat up, people—we've got a graduation to go to."

Aunt Lisa had been coming as often as she could, every few months or so. She had come in March for Mom's one year anniversary, as a surprise. Anna and Eli had gone with Mom to her meeting to celebrate. When Aunt Lisa brought out the cake with her one candle in it, Mom started to cry.

When it was her turn to speak, she said that this was the hardest thing she'd ever done, and that she'd given birth to two ten-pound babies. Everyone laughed. She said that she woke up every day relieved not to be hungover, to know where she was, where her children were. This year, she said, she had to learn how to do everything sober that she knew how to do drunk. She had to learn how to be a mom sober, how to be a sister, how to be a worker. She said she tried very hard to accept her past, but that most days she still wished she could have a do-over. She said that her girls didn't keep her sober—that wasn't their job, but man, they made sobriety worth it, even on bad days, even on their bad days, she'd trade in every good drunk day for a bad sober one with them. People clapped. Anna cried. They went to the diner for root beer floats and curly fries.

The Middletown High auditorium was oddly grand. Plush velvet chairs, lighted walkways, the best air conditioning in the school. Some alum had felt starved of an arts education and donated the money for the theater. No one had donated money for arts education, though; so mostly the theater went unused except for a once-a-year play, weekly assemblies, and graduation.

The lights went down, and the music started. As Anna walked by in the procession, Mom, Aunt Lisa, Javi, and Eli all stood and cheered for her. Anna grimaced, but then she smiled, blew a kiss from her black-lipsticked-lips. Goth girl does graduation, Javi had joked over dinner—her black cap, black gown, black hair, black lipstick. Eli watched Anna cross the stage, seeing her future roll out in front of her. She would never say it herself, but Eli knew Anna was scared. That was okay. Anna scared was Anna invincible, scrambling up to the top of the jungle gym.

That night, after tears and hugs and see-you-this-summers, after Javi, Jason, Jason's parents, Aunt Lisa, Eli, Anna, Mom, John, his wife, and their kids piled into the diner for sundaes, the house was quiet. Aunt Lisa was snoring on the couch, Mom in her room. Eli had gotten into bed, but she wasn't sleeping. The bed was too hot, and then too cold. She opened the window. She closed it. She lay back down. Anna came in without knocking, without speaking. She put one hand on Eli's shoulder to balance as she got into the bed.

"It's okay, PB," she said. "We're okay."

And they slept like spoons until morning.

ACKNOWLEDGMENTS

Writing a book in the years between having a newborn and the onset of a pandemic means there are more people to thank than I can possibly fit in an acceptable amount of space. There is no book without Arthur Levine. I do not know how you see, always, what I'm reaching for and know exactly how to get me on the map towards it. Thank you for loving Eli with your whole heart, and seeing her from the very first sentence. We're both so lucky to have you. All of the folks on the Levine Querido team have been incredible cheerleaders with incredible kindness. Special thanks to Meghan McCullough for sifting through every one of my sentence fragments and comma splices until they made sense, and coming up with brilliant fixes throughout.

Molly Ker Hawn, I don't know, ever, what makes you put up with me. Thank you for your extraordinary agenting, and your equal (and hefty) wells of funny and patient.

Every person who has a small child, a full-time job, and likes to write books should be so lucky as to work for the huge-hearted, hilarious and wise Elizabeth Hannan.

An enormous thank you to my mother, Amy Bloom, for giving us a home, a haven, and a great many hands to get through the school year and write this thing at the same time.

The first time we talked about this book was the day Zora was born. You told me I wouldn't write it quickly, but that I would write it well and just to keep going. I'm so glad I still listen to you. An obvious and profound thank you to my sister Caitlin for many, many, many hours in all types of water *together*.

Jasmine, thank you for finding so many ways to distract Z from the question, "Where's Mama?" Thank you, as always, for making sure that my characters always have the right song playing. Thank you for making me get back in the ring, always.

Some Notes on This Book's Production

The art for the jacket was created by Charlotte Strick and Claire Williams Martinez of Strick&Williams. It uses found elements and textures that were manipulated and collaged together in Photoshop. For the lettering, they hand-traced Flama Semibold and set it in italic to suggest the speed at which the novel's main characters are travelling along on their crumbling, uncared for pastry-highway.

The body text was set by Westchester Publishing Services in Danbury, CT, in Sabon Roman. Designed by Jan Tschichold in 1964, the Sabon font family is a fresh take on Claude Garamond's classical Roman. The title "Sabon" honors Jacques Sabon, a student of Claude Garamond. The display is set in Flama Semibold, designed by Mário Feliciano in 2008. A friendly, geometric sans serif, the Flama font family was originally designed for signage and quickly became an editorial favorite.

Production was supervised by Leslie Cohen and Freesia Blizard
Book jacket and case designed by Strick&Williams
Book interiors designed by Christine Kettner
Edited by Arthur A. Levine

LEVINE QUERIDO